# BARB

Harlequin Presen
Charlotte Lamb w
Barbary Wharf.

In this fascinating saga, you'll experience all the intrigue and glamour of the international world of journalism. You'll watch the inner workings of a newsroom, share the secrets discussed behind closed doors, travel to the most thrilling cities in the world. Join the players in this high-stakes game as they gamble for the biggest prize of all—true love.

You've met Nick Caspian and Gina Tyrrell, whose dramatic story of passion and heartache unfolds throughout this series. You watched as Hazel Forbes and Piet van Leyden fell in love. And you cheered when Roz Amery and Daniel Bruneille's clashes ignited the sparks of their relationship. Now join Irena Olivero and Esteban Sebastian and discover why secrets of the past threaten their promising future.

Don't miss these unforgettable romantic adventures each month in Harlequin Presents—the bestselling romance fiction series in the world.

The Editors

# THE SENTINEL

## SENTINEL JOURNALIST TAKEN HOSTAGE IN HIJACKING

LONDON—Sources at the *Sentinel* have confirmed that Roz Amery, daughter of renowned journalist Desmond Amery, is on board the British Airways jet hijacked shortly after takeoff from Rome yesterday. Authorities have not revealed whether the plane has been allowed to land in Cyprus as per the terrorists' demands. It is not known if any passengers have been injured; the terrorists have promised a one-by-one massacre if their demands for political asylum are not met by noon today.

Ms. Amery is a foreign correspondent with the *Sentinel*. It is feared that the hijackers will consider Ms. Amery a threat to security and use her as a retaliatory example to others on board and to authorities on the ground.

Negotiations continue for the release of the hostages.

## WEDDING BELLS AT BARBARY WHARF

LONDON—Internationally acclaimed Dutch architect Piet van Leyden and Hazel Forbes, executive secretary to *Sentinel* chief Nick Caspian, have announced their engagement. Mr. van Leyden and Ms. Forbes met during the *Sentinel*'s move to the Barbary Wharf complex. A spring wedding is planned.

## DES AMERY TO HEAD PARIS DESK

LONDON—Veteran newsman Desmond Amery has been named Paris correspondent by the *Sentinel*'s editorial committee. Mr. Amery, who has recently made Paris his home, was persuaded out of retirement. Foreign Affairs Chief Editor Daniel Bruneille said he is delighted that Mr. Amery has agreed to become a member of the *Sentinel*'s foreign affairs department. He joins his daughter, Roz Amery, who is already a foreign correspondent with the paper.

Harlequin Presents first edition December 1992
ISBN 0-373-11513-X

Original hardcover edition published in 1992
by Mills & Boon Limited

TOO CLOSE FOR COMFORT

# Charlotte Lamb

## Too Close For Comfort

### BARBARY WHARF

# Harlequin Books

TORONTO • NEW YORK • LONDON
AMSTERDAM • PARIS • SYDNEY • HAMBURG
STOCKHOLM • ATHENS • TOKYO • MILAN
MADRID • WARSAW • BUDAPEST • AUCKLAND

# BARBARY WHARF

For more than one hundred years, London's Fleet Street has been the heartbeat of Britain's major newspaper and magazine industries. But decaying buildings and the high cost of inner-city real estate have forced many companies to relocate dockside, down by the Thames River.

The owner of one such company, Sir George Tyrrell, had a dream, a vision of leading his newspaper, the *Sentinel*, into the twenty-first century with a huge, ultramodern complex called Barbary Wharf. But without additional money and time, the dream—and perhaps even the newspaper—will die.

Enter Nick Caspian, international media tycoon. The man with all the money, desire and the means to take over the *Sentinel*. But will he change the paper beyond recognition? Will he change the life of Gina Tyrrell, a woman who understands his desires?

And what of the people behind the scenes at the *Sentinel*? Although passion rages between Irena Olivero, the beautiful Spanish translator, and Esteban Sebastian, Irena knows that Esteban has a past filled with secrecy and shame. Like Gina, she must compete for the man she loves, but can Irena compete against such a powerful ghost? And does any of it matter if her beloved half sister, Roz Amery, is not released by her hijackers . . . ?

# BARBARY WHARF

## CAST OF CHARACTERS

*Irena Olivero*—Des Amery's illegitimate daughter; Roz Amery's half sister. Irena has left her humble country home in Spain to join the *Sentinel*'s translation department. She is determined to make her mark in the world.

*Esteban Sebastian*—The *Sentinel*'s dashing marketing director who has a reputation for being the company's chief heartthrob.

*Gina Tyrrell*—The young widow of Sir George Tyrrell's beloved grandson. Devastated by her husband's death, she devoted herself entirely to Sir George's well-being. And now she will devote herself entirely to his paper, the *Sentinel*.

*Nick Caspian*—International media tycoon with playboy reputation. Owns and operates newspapers all over Europe, and has now set his sights on Britain—starting with the *Sentinel*.

*Roz Amery*—Foreign affairs correspondent. The daughter of Des Amery, an internationally acclaimed journalist, she is fiercely ambitious. Half sister to Irena Olivero.

*Daniel Bruneille*—Chief foreign affairs editor. Rules the department with an iron fist. Fiery and temperamental, he is nevertheless admired and respected—and much loved by Roz Amery.

# CHAPTER ONE

DES saw her off at the airport. An experienced traveller, he had made sure she carried all her relevant documents in a leather case, which he checked before they left for Charles de Gaulle. 'Passport, air ticket, traveller's cheques, money...' he murmured, ticking them all off on the list he had insisted she made so that she wouldn't forget anything. Sometimes she felt he thought she was still at school.

After she had checked in at the departure desk, he looked down at her, searchingly. 'You're paler than usual.' Irena always had a pale complexion. 'You're not nervous, are you?'

'A little,' she confessed, her wide grey eyes anxious. 'I'm afraid I'll forget all my English once I get to London, and just stand there in the airport tongue-tied and stupid!'

'Roz speaks fluent French; she'll meet you right outside Customs,' he reminded her. 'Even if every word of English escapes you, no need to panic, it will soon come back. Within half an hour you'll be chattering away to Roz without thinking.'

She gave him a rueful little smile. 'You're more confident than I am, Des!' She always used his first name; she had only known he was her father for such a short time, and somehow it seemed more natural to call him Des, the way her half-sister, Roz, always did.

Des gently touched her cheek, his eyes tender. At times when he looked at this girl he felt his life tilt wildly, back

7

to his own childhood, and the mother he had loved so much. Heredity was unpredictable in the way it worked. His other daughter, Roz, looked like him—she had inherited his dark hair and blue eyes, although in him the colours were fading year by year, his hair silvering over and his blue eyes turning almost grey. But Irena was the very image of his mother as a girl: her great shimmering eyes, her long, smooth brown hair, the sweet shyness of her smile. And it wasn't merely a physical resemblance. This child he had not even known he had fathered until so recently worried him, because he remembered how fragile and vulnerable his mother had always been.

'You'll enjoy yourself once you get there,' he assured her. 'Roz will look after you.' He had never had to worry about Roz; she had always been strong and sure of herself. They were both so different, his two girls, he was proud of both of them, loved them both, but he knew it was Roz who was the most like himself.

Irena gave a start. 'Oh, they're calling my flight! Where's my bag? I'll be late!'

'Calm down,' Des said. 'That's only the first call. You have plenty of time, so long as you don't go to Duty Free. Just go straight to the gate your flight leaves from— OK?'

She nodded, turning to run, then came back and stood on tiptoe to kiss his cheek because she was a head shorter. '*Au 'voir*, Des, see you when you get back from Vietnam, and take care, won't you? Don't take any risks.'

He grinned. 'I've no intentions of taking any risks!'

She eyed him doubtfully, knowing his reputation as one of the most daring foreign correspondents, but there was no time to say any more, so she kissed him again, and then vanished in the rush of other passengers with a final wave, to make her way up the futuristic glass tubes which led to the departure deck.

Only as the aircraft took off from Charles de Gaulle airport did she look down on the grey blur of Paris far below and feel tears prick her eyes. She was going to miss Des, and she felt a surge of loneliness.

If he had not decided to accept an invitation to tour Vietnam, North and South, and write a series of articles on the changes which had happened in both in the years since the end of the long war between them, she would not be on her way to London, she would have stayed in Paris with Des, and probably taken a summer job until the university autumn term began at the Sorbonne. As Paris correspondent he was the ideal person to write the articles, however, Vietnam having originally been French-owned and being still a subject very important politically to the French people today.

Roz had been staying with them when Des announced his plans, and had asked, 'What will you do, Irena, if Des is away all summer? Go home to Spain?'

'For a couple of weeks, just to see my mother and brothers,' Irena had nodded. 'But I need to earn some money during the vacation, and I can't do that on the farm. They need help, but I couldn't let them pay me, because they only just make enough to live on themselves!'

Their farm was really nothing more than a white-washed cottage: five small rooms and a barn set on a slope above their stony, arid acres, which could not support any crop except a few vines. They kept animals, though even so not in any great numbers. They had some horses, because in winter snows a horse could go where a tractor or a four-wheel drive car could not, and, anyway, her brothers loved horses, and each had one of their own; they kept a couple of sows which annually produced between them à couple of dozen piglets for sale at market, some hens, for their eggs, which when they stopped laying were killed and sold, or, if they were too old and tough to sell, put in the pot and stewed for the family, a flock of small, brown goats, whose milk they drank or made into cheese or yoghurt, and a larger flock of thin, wiry sheep which wandered the hills, from pasture to pasture, as the grass grew green and then was bleached by the hot Andalucían sun.

It was labour-intensive farming, there was always work to do, and her mother worked hard, but not as hard as the two boys, Ramón, who was nearly eighteen now, but looked older, and Miguel, who was sixteen. They could have been twins, black-haired, black-eyed, broad and muscled, except that Ramón was a few inches taller. 'My little bulls,' their father had called them, proudly, as they argued and fought through their childhood.

It had been a bitter shock to Irena when, after the death of the man she had always called her father, her mother had told her she was another man's child, and only a half-sister to Ramón and Miguel.

Her mother, Grazia, had met the famous journalist Des Amery in London when she worked as nanny to his motherless little girl, Roz. Des had been recently bereaved, and very unhappy; Grazia was warm-hearted and fell in love with his sadness and need. Irena had been the result, although Grazia had not known she was pregnant until after she had returned home to Spain.

She had never told Des; instead she had married a man she had known all her life, a poor farmer in the Andalucían foothills. Ambrosio Olivero had been a good man, and a loving father; Irena had been stricken when her mother told her the truth about her parentage. But now, thanks largely to Des and Roz, it had all been re-solved inside her.

She could still love Ambrosio, who in her mind would always be her father, yet also love her real father, Des, without disloyalty to Ambrosio. She had turned against her mother for a while, but that, too, was long over. Nobody was to blame for what had happened, she saw that now. Des had helped her to understand, telling her that these things happened to people, they made mis-takes, they were reckless, they got hurt, that was the muddled nature of being human.

She often felt guilty about her comparatively luxurious life in Paris while her mother and half-brothers worked all the hours in the day to keep the family farm going. It was a hard, struggling existence and although she now lived with Des she still felt part of the Olivero world; she wanted to help them with money, knowing they badly needed it.

When Roz suggested, 'Come and work as a translator at the *Sentinel*—we carry a permanent team to read through foreign papers and pick out the more interesting stories,' Irena had jumped at the idea. She would be able to send money home as well as support herself throughout the summer.

Roz had talked to Daniel Bruneille, the foreign news editor, who would be Irena's immediate boss, and in an amazingly short time it had all been decided. Irena would work at the newspaper and would live with Roz, in the large riverside flat she shared with Daniel. They were not married, but she was sure they would be, in time.

She looked down on the patchwork quilt which was the countryside of the Pas de Calais, delighted by the changing colours of the landscape below; the yellow of wheat, the green of pasture, the white ribbons of the roads. This was very different countryside from the one in which she had grown up, in parched Spain. Suddenly the land ended and the sea began, the sun glittering on blue waves. Not long now before they landed in London! Irena stood up to make her way to the lavatory; she must wash and renew her make-up before they arrived.

She had the window seat, there was an empty seat next to her, and the aisle seat was occupied by a tall, bronzed man with a Mediterranean look, who had ignored her throughout the flight. He was absorbed in a folder of papers, his long legs stretched out blocking her way. Irena halted next to him and waited for him to move.

'*Excusez-mois, monsieur,*' she said, and he started in surprise, his grip on the folder slackening for a second. The folder began to slide out of his hand, and papers spilled in all directions.

He muttered something harsh and indistinct, hurriedly grabbing at them. Irena went down on her knees to pick up those on the floor, and he turned on her.

'Leave them!' he said in Spanish, making her freeze, wide-eyed. She had spoken French to him, and she knew her French was good, almost accentless—how had he known she was Spanish? While she stared at him he gave her a brief, frowning look, as if noticing her startled expression. 'Please don't touch them!' he said in slow, thickly accented French, and Irena understood then. He hadn't guessed she was Spanish, after all. He was Spanish himself!

She obeyed silently, standing up again, and while he was preoccupied with gathering up his papers she took a closer look at him, and wryly decided she should have guessed his nationality. Not merely because he was tall, with black hair, deeply tanned olive skin, and black eyes, but because of the sombre, almost brooding air he carried around. Spanish men were usually grave, reserved, always aware of their dignity. Even her brothers, who were not yet even men, would take on that solemn look. It was an outward sign of their masculinity, their sense of the gravity of being men!

He stood up again, moving out into the aisle and gesturing with cold courtesy to her to pass, and, very flushed, she hurried away with a murmured apology in French. For some reason she didn't think she should tell him she was Spanish. She had a strong feeling he would interpret it as an attempt to get into conversation, and that he would snub her.

She took her time, brushing her long, smooth hair until it gleamed, renewing her lipstick and dusting powder on her faintly shiny nose, and as she returned to her seat heard the stewardess's flat English voice announcing that they would be landing soon at Heathrow.

A cramp of excitement hit Irena's stomach. She was nervous about meeting strangers or travelling; she was intensely self-conscious and unsure of herself, very shy.

But she was looking forward to seeing her half-sister again. She and Roz had never really been alone before; Des and Daniel had always been around and somehow when men were present the atmosphere was different. Maybe she and Roz would finally get to know each other? She hoped so.

The plane landed smoothly and taxied to its docking bay, and Irena began to gather up her hand luggage, then got up to retrieve her jacket out of the overhead locker. She had to stand on tiptoe, her body stretched to its absolute limit as she groped around inside the locker. Her tall neighbour was standing behind her.

'*Permettez…*' he murmured, with a dry irony, his body almost touching hers as he reached over her head and without any difficulty pulled out her jacket.

'*Merci, monsieur*,' she said, risking an upward look out of her soft grey eyes.

He inclined his head, his face impassive now, turned away to collect his own belongings from the seat where he had placed them, and walked off down the aisle, leaving Irena to follow in his wake. She watched the stewardess giving him an inviting smile, and wondered if he had smiled back—if he could smile!

His long legs covered the ground much faster than Irena could, so he was out of sight by the time she got to Passport Control, but when she arrived at Baggage Reclaim he was waiting there, pacing impatiently to and fro, looking at his watch. A second later, though, her suitcase came up and she grabbed it and walked towards the exit labelled 'Nothing to Declare'. As she came through the swing doors she halted to look around at the crowd waiting out there. This was where Roz should be standing. Where was she?

Irena's anxious grey eyes moved from face to face, but there was no sign of her sister. While she stood there, in the doorway, there was a short sigh behind her, and a familiar deep voice said, '*Mademselle… je vous en prie… je suis pressé…*'

She almost groaned as she moved out of his way. Wouldn't you know it would be him? '*Désolée, monsieur*,' she mumbled, and at that instant saw Daniel and with a sigh of relief ran towards him, almost tripping over her suitcase.

'There you are,' Daniel said in French, and bent to kiss her, on both cheeks, because they were almost related; one day soon Daniel would be her brother-in-law.

'Where's Roz?' she asked, looking behind him without seeing her sister.

'She was in Rome yesterday; her flight should have arrived an hour ago, but the plane developed some sort of engine problem. As soon as she realised she wouldn't make it to meet you in time, she rang me and I hopped into a cab. Roz was having kittens, imagining you stranded and getting into a panic!' He looked down at her, laughing. 'Of course, you would have coped, got yourself into a taxi—but your big sister doesn't believe it.'

Irena smiled back at him, thinking how lucky Roz was to have a man like him. Daniel was as sexy and exciting as a film star. She was a little in awe of him—he was clever, and could be cuttingly sarcastic, and so full of energy that you felt he might give you an electric shock if he touched you. Roz seemed to find it easy enough to cope with him, but then Roz was quite formidable, herself. They made a striking pair.

'It's very kind of you to go to all this trouble to meet me,' she shyly said. 'I was very glad to see a familiar face. But of course I would have managed somehow if nobody had turned up. When I was still not quite eighteen I got myself from one side of Spain to the other by train, and on to Paris!'

'But the hard part was getting from the railway station in Paris to your hotel, right?' Daniel teased, grinning as he took her case from her and slid an arm round her to guide her towards the exit.

'Paris traffic is bad,' she agreed, frowning as a thought occurred to her. 'Aren't we going to wait for Roz?'

'Her plane isn't arriving for several hours; I checked with the airport information desk. That's too long for us to wait. Don't worry, Roz won't mind—she'll take a taxi when she does get here, and join us at the flat.'

There was only one man waiting at the taxi rank. Irena recognised the broad shoulders and long, slim back, and her heart sank. Him, again!

Cheerfully, Daniel said, 'If the roads are clear, we should get to our flat in an hour. But it can take two hours, in heavy traffic. Are you tired, you poor little poppet? You're very pale.'

'I'm fine,' she said as a taxi arrived and the man in front of them stepped forward to claim it. Daniel watched, then suddenly did a double take. 'Esteban!'

The other man turned with obvious reluctance, and without any show of surprise, making Irena certain that he had recognised Daniel some time ago without acknowledging him. 'Hello, Daniel.'

'I didn't spot you before,' Daniel said, and the other man shrugged.

'That's OK, you had other things on your mind.' His cold eyes briefly touched on Irena, and Daniel's white teeth showed in an amused grin.

'So I did.' He sketched a gesture between them. 'Irena, this is Esteban Sebastian, the marketing director of the *Sentinel*, and one of your own countrymen—Esteban, Irena is coming to work in the translation section for the summer; she's Spanish, too, by an odd coincidence.'

Esteban half bowed, chillingly polite. 'How do you do?' he said in English.

She muttered something husky and incoherent, not quite meeting his eyes.

The taxi driver had put Esteban's case into the taxi. He got back behind his wheel and leaned over, impatiently asking, 'Well, is one of you coming with me?'

Esteban climbed into the cab, looked back to ask curtly, 'Would you like to share my taxi?'

Luckily, at that instant, another taxi drove towards them. Daniel gave Irena a quick look, accurately read her expression, and said, 'Thanks for the offer, Esteban, but we'll take the next one. We haven't had a real chance to talk yet.'

Esteban Sebastian's hard mouth twisted. 'Of course,' he said, in that deep, remote voice. 'See you in the office.' His taxi drove off, and Irena sighed with relief. Daniel handed her case to the second taxi driver while she was climbing into the back of the cab.

'Do I gather you didn't take to our Esteban?' he asked as he joined her a second or two later.

'He wasn't very friendly,' she stammered, her face averted. She didn't like to tell Daniel about the silly incident on the plane, or her instinctive awareness that Esteban Sebastian had taken an instant dislike to her. Some things were too intangible to be explained. Daniel was a logical, rational man; he would dismiss her feelings as mere imagination.

Daniel's eyebrows lifted, but he dropped the subject with a light shrug. 'You travel light—won't you need more than one case of clothes if you're going to be here for seven weeks? I know Roz would need a whole van load!'

'I don't have any more clothes,' Irena said shyly, blushing, and Daniel looked incredulous.

'What a confession from someone who lives in Paris! Well, we must see what we can do about that while you're here. It will give Roz a kick to take you shopping. London is a great fashion centre, too, you know, especially for classic English clothes, or the latest casual gear.'

Irena was horrified, and in an embarrassed voice muttered, 'Please, don't suggest it to Roz, Daniel. I can't afford to spend money on clothes, and, anyway, I have all I need.'

Daniel flicked a look over her in her cool turquoise cotton suit, his dark eyes appreciative. 'That's a delightful outfit—where did you buy that?'

'I made it myself.'

'Really?' He looked her over again, his face impressed. 'Aren't you a clever girl?'

Her blush deepened. 'I make most of my clothes myself on an old second-hand sewing-machine I bought in a Paris flea market.' She had bought the material in a sale, half-price, and designed the suit herself, too: a drop-waisted, flowing dress, with a matching jacket. It was much cheaper than buying her clothes from a shop.

Today, London traffic was light. It only took an hour to reach Roz's and Daniel's flat in a new block by the Thames, a short walk from Barbary Wharf. Daniel pointed out the futuristic complex as they drove past, and Irena stared, eyes wide.

The smoked glass windows glittered in the sun, the octagonal building was reflected in the dark, flowing water of the river beside which it stood. There was something faintly barbaric about the structure, a hint of a fortress, of something hidden behind high walls, and Irena shivered.

Daniel gave her a shrewd sideways look. 'Don't look so panic-stricken. You'll soon feel at home.'

'I hope so.' Her voice had a fatalistic fall. What difference would it make whether or not she enjoyed working there? She needed the money and had been very lucky to get this job.

A few minutes later the taxi dropped them at the modern apartment block which had been built at around the same time as Barbary Wharf, and they rode up in the lift to the third floor. Daniel unlocked the front door and stood back to let her walk inside before following her with her case.

'First, let's go and see the room you'll be using,' he said, leading the way down a narrow corridor and showing her each room they passed. Her room was at the far end; he pushed open the door and Irena stood staring around, delighted by the light and space of the square room, which was simply furnished in a modern style.

The walls were painted white, the carpet and curtains were a sunny lemon, and the furniture was golden pine. There were enormous windows through which she saw a panoramic view of the river. One wall held continuous wardrobe space with fitted, sliding doors, something Irena had never seen before. There was even a small armchair facing a TV set and a row of books on a shelf of a bedside cabinet.

'It's beautiful!' Irena said breathlessly, and Daniel smiled.

'I'm glad you like it! I'll leave you to unpack, and get used to your new home. If you need me, I'll be in the kitchen. Roz shouldn't be long. Oh, by the way—tonight, we're eating out, at Barbary Wharf, Pierre's restaurant. You'll love it.' He paused, then said gently, 'One other thing, Irena—I know we all find it easier to speak French, but from now on you must practise your English, you know. This is London, and that is why you're here—to improve your English.'

She blushed, nodded and said carefully in English, 'I know, and I will use it from now on.'

'Good girl,' he said, and then the door closed and she was alone. She gave a deep sigh and went over to the window to stare out, hardly believing she was here—there was the Thames, running softly by, and opposite her was a huddle of tower blocks, grey roofs and spires that was some part of London's massive sprawl. It was all so strange, so alien—Irena wished she was back in Paris. She would never fit in here!

Gina Tyrrell was standing at her window in the oak-panelled office in Barbary Wharf at that moment, watching the late afternoon light gleam on the Thames, too, while she talked over her shoulder.

'Yes, why not ask her to the wedding, Hazel? It would please Roz, and I'm sure you're going to like Irena, she's so shy and sweet ...'

'Nothing like Roz, then,' Hazel said, grinning.

Gina laughed. 'Well, I don't suppose Roz would want to be called shy and sweet, anyway. No, you would never guess they had the same father! Irena doesn't even look like Des Amery. I suppose she takes after her mother.'

'Does she want to be a reporter, too?' Hazel was filing while she talked, her small hands deft and precise as they slotted folders into place.

Gina shrugged. 'No idea, but I don't think she's the type. She is far too sensitive, I'd say, but she's good at languages, like Roz and Des. That's what she's studying at university in Paris. But it would be fun for her to go to an English wedding, and it's very kind of you to think of it, Hazel.'

'Well, I expect she would feel left out, if I didn't ask her, as Roz and Daniel are going.'

'Is your wedding dress finished yet?'

'I'm having the final fitting next week.'

At that moment they both heard a door slam, and Gina's head lifted sharply. She and Hazel exchanged looks.

'He's back.' Nick Caspian had been involved in lengthy meetings all afternoon with one of the major print unions and from the sound of it he had come back in a temper, which wasn't unusual. He had been having trouble with most of the British unions since he took over the *Sentinel*; partly because he was trying to rationalise staff working-hours and pay, to fall into line with the conditions operating on the Continent, at his other European newspapers, and partly because the British workers were far more inclined to distrust their proprietor's motives and to fight him wherever and whenever they could.

Gina walked hurriedly towards her desk, to collect her belongings. The desk had belonged to Sir George Tyrrell, the grandfather of her husband, James, who had died six years ago. When the *Sentinel* moved to Barbary Wharf from Fleet Street, the valuable antique leather-topped desk had been in Sir George's office, but when he died and Nick Caspian took over he had taken over the old man's office, too. Gina had bitterly resented the idea of Nick sitting at that desk. She blamed Nick Caspian for the old man's death; if he hadn't tried to get complete control of the paper Sir George might still be alive, and seeing him behind that desk was a visible sign of Nick's victory, the old man's death and defeat.

When Nick had persuaded her to stay on at the *Sentinel*, however, he had had the desk moved into her office—a thoughtful gesture which hadn't lessened her distrust of him. Nick had known how she felt; that was the disturbing fact. Gina did not want Nick Caspian to know so much about her.

'I'm off,' she said huskily, rather pale now. She avoided meeting Nick whenever she could, which was easy enough most of the year, because he spent so much time away from London. His international publishing house owned newspapers in every capital in Europe, and when he was abroad, at one of his other newspapers, weeks could go by before she saw him, but for the past fortnight he had been in London and Gina had been racked with tension. Nick had a devastating effect on her nerves and this afternoon she was too tired, after a long, hard week, to feel up to facing him if he was in one of his tempers.

She was too late to escape, however; just as she was leaving, Nick Caspian walked into their office. He gave Gina a comprehensive look, sweeping from her elegantly dressed russet hair, down over her slim figure in an amber silk shirt-waister dress to her long legs. His face was cool, but some comment was intended and Gina knew it, gritting her teeth.

'Clock-watching?' he mocked.

'I've got a date tonight!'

His jawline tightened. 'Philip?'

'Yes,' she murmured, her lashes veiling her almond-shaped green eyes. She tried not to look at him at all, but her mind's eye always carried an image of him, which she was matching up now, in brief, nervous flickers, a quick glance then away again, then back, as if making sure there had been no change since she last saw him.

Nick was in his mid to late thirties, very fit; a lean, supple man with long legs and an impatient way of moving with swift and easy strides.

Gina had never yet discovered much about him or his family background, not even where he had been born or brought up. Other newspapers had tried to probe his life, coming up with very little, although she had once read somewhere that his father, Zachariah Caspian, was dead. He never talked about himself or his past and interviewers who asked such questions were coldly cut short.

One thing was obvious: he was distinctly Latin in his colouring, dark and tanned, with an olive skin, although with that went surprisingly clear cool grey eyes which at that moment glittered angrily.

'Well, before you leave I want a word—will you come through to my office?' he barked, then looked at Hazel. 'Are those letters ready for me to sign?'

'Yes, all of them,' she said in her usual tranquil voice, picking up a folder full of the perfectly typed letters she had prepared.

Nick took them from her impatiently and whirled back into his office. Hazel and Gina grimaced at each other, then Gina followed him, closing the door behind her.

Nick was sitting behind his desk, signing the letters with quick, flowing strokes of his gold fountain pen.

'I am in a hurry—is this important?' Gina asked, staying on the other side of the room, near the door.

Nick's dark head didn't lift, nor did his pen falter. 'Yes,' he said with cold insistence. 'I won't be a moment. I want to finish signing these letters so that they can catch today's post.'

Gina looked around the elegant golden-oak panelling, the gentle late afternoon sunlight flowed over it like water in shimmering swirls. Suddenly, she noticed that a portrait of Sir George Tyrrell's father had gone from its accustomed place between the windows, and been replaced by one of a man so short he might have been a dwarf. Or perhaps that was merely the way he sat in his chair: hunched shoulders, chin sunk down on his chest, his eyes brooding on something apparently far away. He was dark-skinned, dark-eyed, his hair grey and very thin, sliding backwards off his forehead.

Nick had finished signing his letters and looked up to watch her staring at the painting.

'My father,' he said curtly, and Gina flicked him a glance.

'Oh.' So that was Zachariah Caspian? Nick didn't look like him, she decided, looking back at the picture.

'It's the best painting of him ever done,' said Nick in a flat voice. 'My mother has had it hanging in her house in San Francisco for years; I didn't think she would ever part with it, but she just sent it to me.'

'Your mother lives in America?' Gina hadn't even known that, had not known if his mother was still alive.

He nodded, drumming his fingertips on the desk as he always did when he was impatient or angry. 'That's what I want to talk to you about. I'm considering branching out into the States, and I thought I'd go over to the west coast to look at the situation out there. I shall take a management study group with me to make an assessment of the potential, or otherwise—and I want you on the team.'

Gina felt her nerves prickling. 'You want me to go to California?' she said slowly, green eyes as wary as a frightened cat's, trying to guess what lay behind the suggestion. 'I wouldn't be any use in assessing the market potential over there; I'm no market expert.'

'You're the one who keeps insisting on joint control, who wants to know what's going on, why decisions are being made,' Nick drawled. 'You can't share management if you never leave London or find out what is going on in the rest of the corporation.'

Gina bit out, 'The Caspian organisation is nothing to do with me. I'm a Tyrrell.'

'You married a Tyrrell,' Nick muttered, his voice angry. 'That doesn't make you one.'

She stared at him with bitter resentment, her eyes fire-bright. It was true, of course, and yet, in another sense, she felt like a Tyrrell; she knew Sir George had learned to think of her as one of his family—that was why he had left her his shares and had wanted her to carry on when he had gone.

'I became a Tyrrell when I married James,' she threw back at Nick, and he got up, pushing back his chair. Gina stiffened, her whole body deeply aware of him. She might hate and despise Nick Caspian but simply being in the same room with him had a catastrophic effect on her; a chemical reaction she couldn't control and barely managed to conceal from him.

'I'm not even discussing it,' she huskily muttered, struggling to stay calm. 'I am only interested in what happens at the *Sentinel*; don't try to involve me in Caspian business.' She turned blindly towards the door, but Nick was already right behind her and he caught her arm in an iron grip.

'Don't you walk out on me, Gina!'

She was really frightened now, but she fought to hide it, snapping at him. 'How many times do I have to tell you that I hate you to touch me?'

'I've got to the point where I don't give a damn if you do,' he muttered, his stare fixed on her parted, trembling lips, and a shudder ran through her. She stared back at him, hardly breathing, the most intense desire ripping her heart, and then the phone on the desk began to ring and Gina started violently.

Nick stood there for a long moment, his eyes not moving from her pale face, then he let go of her and strode back to the desk to lean over and snatch up the phone.

'Yes?' he snarled into it, then listened, his back to Gina, who was so shaky that she couldn't walk out of there quite yet. Her heart was beating so hard that it made her feel sick and her legs were as weak as water.

'What?' Nick said harshly, and she looked across at him, feeling him turn his head to stare at her while he was listening to whatever was being said on the other end of the line.

Gina had a sudden intuition and didn't go yet, waited, watching Nick's hard face. The colour was draining out of it; he was frowning, his eyes dark, his skin grey. What was wrong? Bad news, Gina thought, but what sort of news? Business, or personal? With Nick there rarely seemed to be much of a dividing line between the two.

'You're sure she is on it?' Nick asked, then frowned as the answer came. 'Yes, I see. No, I'll speak to him, myself. Just stay there, and keep me informed of any developments, immediately.'

He put the phone down and turned to look at Gina, his brows heavy, but didn't say anything for a long moment, his lower lip caught between his teeth as if he was working out what to say, or how to say it.

'What is it?' Gina asked, puzzled and disturbed. 'Is something wrong?'

Nick sighed. 'It's Roz,' he said, and Gina's breath caught in shock.

'Roz? She came back from Rome hours ago—she was meeting Irena at Heathrow...'

'The Rome plane was delayed. They had had a bomb warning,' Nick said in a quiet, level voice. 'They searched the plane for hours but found nothing, so the flight took off four hours late.'

Gina was trembling, her face white, her imagination leaping ahead of him in horror, visualising what she could not bear to think about. 'Oh, no...no...not Roz...'

Nick quickly said, 'She isn't dead, Gina, it wasn't a bomb.'

She gave a long, relieved sigh, then her green eyes focused on him intently. 'Then...what...?'

Nick sighed. 'The warning had been in English and the operator in Rome must have misunderstood it. It wasn't a bomb, it was terrorists, aboard the plane.'

'Terrorists!' Gina bit her lip so hard that she felt blood trickle into her mouth.

'They've hijacked the plane and are forcing the pilot to fly to Cyprus,' Nick said flatly. 'That was Ben Winter, one of our news reporters. He had just arrived at Nicosia airport, from London, for a fortnight's holiday, and he was queuing in the terminal to sign for a hire car he had booked when suddenly there were police and soldiers everywhere and everyone was ordered out, told to leave the area immediately. Of course, Ben refused to go, and identified himself with his Press card, so he got the story before anyone else. He says it's hard to find out exactly who these people are, or what is happening, but there seem to be two or three terrorists. When he discovered it was a flight from Rome to London, he remembered Daniel telling him Roz was coming home from Rome today.'

# CHAPTER TWO

GINA'S legs felt weak under her; she sank down on the nearest chair, her hands gripped in her lap to stop them shaking. 'But...but...why hasn't the news broken earlier, if the plane was hijacked several hours ago? Why hasn't it come in from the agencies?'

'There has been a media black-out, at the Cyprus end, Ben says. No statement was being made until they could confirm positively that there were terrorists on board. He thinks they don't know exactly what is going on yet, so they aren't talking. He only got as much as he did because he just happened to be on the spot. He suspects they may try to refuse landing rights.'

Gina drew a horrified breath. 'But...will there be enough fuel for the plane to go on elsewhere? What if the terrorists turn nasty and...? Oh, my God, Roz...'

'Don't let your imagination run riot,' Nick said, watching her with a frown. 'Until we have a clearer picture of what is behind all this, try to stay calm, Gina.'

She flared up at once, her green eyes angry. 'Easy for you to say! Roz isn't your oldest friend! You aren't directly involved!'

'I've known Roz for years,' Nick snapped. 'Do you think I'm not deeply worried about her safety?'

He turned his back on her and strode back to the desk, picked up an internal phone. 'I'd better ring Daniel.' His mouth was level, reined hard. 'I don't look forward to breaking the news. Thank God he's trained to handle crises; he's going to need all his training to deal with this.'

Gina looked down at her hands, twisting and turning in her lap. The news would hit Daniel hard, in spite of his training. He had been a tough foreign correspondent for years, used to danger and tragedy, but that was the past. He had changed beyond all recognition since he and Roz began living together. Happiness had made him a different man; warmer, more approachable, easier to like. If anything happened to Roz it would tear Daniel apart.

Nick was talking curtly into the phone; she began to listen, frowning at his tone. He couldn't be talking to Daniel, surely! 'Where? Oh, I see. No, I'll ring him at home.' He put the phone down and looked at her. 'Daniel had a call from Roz to say she couldn't meet Irena because her plane had been delayed, so Daniel shot off to Heathrow several hours ago.' He picked up a large, leather-bound book and began flicking through the pages. 'I must have Daniel's home phone number in here,' he said.

She flatly supplied the number from memory, and he put the book down after a brief glance at her. 'Thank you.' He began to dial, saying, 'He should be back home by now, but I don't imagine he will have heard the news yet.'

One of the other phones on the desk began to ring at that instant, and Nick picked it up while he was waiting for someone to answer in Daniel's flat. 'Yes, what is it?' he impatiently said, then, 'Oh, hello, Fabien—yes, I know, we've heard, Ben rang us before he was put through to the foreign desk. I'm ringing Daniel myself, now. Leave it to me to break the news. Yes, Ben can handle it for the moment, but you'll have to send someone out there.' He frowned. 'There's no answer from Daniel's flat; maybe he hasn't gone straight home? He may be waiting at Heathrow for Roz. Look, I'll keep ringing him. He'll want to go out there when he hears the news. I'll make sure my private jet is available to fly him to Cyprus. It will be easier; they've shut Nicosia airport down, so they'll have to land elsewhere on the island. We'll send another reporter with him; we can't ask Daniel to cover this story, and it wouldn't be fair on Ben to ask him to work when he should be on holiday. No, I don't mind who goes, pick someone yourself. I'll be in touch when I've got hold of Daniel.'

He hung up on Fabien, waited another moment, then hung up the other phone. 'Where the hell can Daniel have got to?'

'Maybe he's heard, and is on his way here?' suggested Gina, but Nick's mouth twisted.

'If I know Daniel, he would be on his way back to the airport to get the first plane to Cyprus. No, he can't have heard—but where is he?'

'Showing Irena the sights?' suggested Gina with a sigh.

Roz was thinking about Daniel, too; an image of his face filling her mind, so that she had to bite her lip to stifle a groan of anguish. Would she ever see him again? She had wasted so many years of quarrelling with him, fighting how she felt, and now it might all be over.

She was in acute discomfort, crouched in her seat on the plane, her hands linked behind her head to keep them at all time in view of the two terrorists armed with pistols and hand grenades who stood at the front of the plane watching the rest of the passengers with jumpy, flickering eyes. How had they got their weapons on board? she thought, remembering the story the Rome authorities had given out. Engine trouble had caused the long delay in taking off, they had been told—only now did it become clear that there had been some sort of warning, and the plane had been thoroughly searched—so how had these men smuggled their weapons on to the plane?

A middle-aged woman in the seat next to her was crying silently with closed eyes, tears creeping from under her lids, making a shining track down her pale, sweating face. Roz dared not speak to her; they had been forbidden to utter a sound. She couldn't put an arm round her or try to offer comfort; if she tried to lower her hands she might be shot.

She knew the odds. There was a very strong chance that this was her last day on earth. The three men who had taken over the plane were hyped up for this, their nerves like live wires. If anyone said the wrong thing, did the wrong thing, it could mean death for everyone on board. There was a hair-trigger atmosphere on the plane, especially since they had stopped travelling at a high altitude, had come down through the clouds and begun flying round and round in a circle above an island.

The passengers had been told nothing except that to disobey their captors would be dangerous. Nobody had dared ask questions after the shouted orders were underlined by one man pointing a pistol at a child's head. The mother had turned white and almost passed out. The father's face had gone old and grey. The child had begun to cry, turning his face into his mother's arm, and the gunman had bared his teeth in a humourless grin.

'OK. You get it.' His voice was a rough snarl, expecting no reply; none was necessary, they all got the point.

Out of the corner of her eye Roz could see the grey rocky hills, the green valleys, the rough indentations of an island coastline. A Greek island? Or were they still near Italy? Was this Sardinia? Sicily? No, they had been flying for too long. It had to be further off. It looks familiar, she thought... I've been here, haven't I? And then it came to her. Cyprus. They were trying to land in Cyprus.

The plane suddenly stopped flying in a holding pattern and dipped one wing to change direction, beginning to lose height a moment later. The gunmen stiffened, muttered to each other, then the one who had threatened the child earlier turned and screamed at the passengers in thick English, 'All go to back of plane... Get down, on floor, all get down at back of plane! Keeping hands on heads. All hands on heads or I shoot!'

There was panic as the passengers scrambled up and ran to the back of the plane, then lay down on their faces, their hands still linked behind their heads. Roz felt herself shaking and fought to stay calm. If she was going to die, then... then she would be dead quickly. At least it wouldn't be a lingering death. That would be far worse. Any pain would be bad, but brief.

The plane banked sharply downwards, as if they were crashing down out of the sky, falling fast. Some of the women screamed; a man was praying in a low, mumbled voice. Roz lay still and made herself concentrate on memorising everything that happened. That was what Des would do, or Daniel. This was the scoop of her life. If she survived, she would need to remember every single detail of these moments. If she didn't... well, then, she didn't.

When she had unpacked and rested for a while, Irena joined Daniel in the little sitting-room to wait for Roz to arrive. They each sipped an aperitif while they talked, their eyes on the clock.

'I'll ring the airport information desk and see if I can find out what is holding her up,' Daniel finally said, frowning a little anxiously. He took some time to get through, and after a short conversation hung up, his face irritated. 'Further delays, they say. They didn't seem too sure what was wrong. I asked if the plane had actually taken off, and the girl sounded very vague even about that. Further delays was all she knew. It might be weather en route, she said, and told me to ring back later when they may know more.'

'Oh, poor Roz,' Irena said. 'I hate sitting around in airports.'

'I can't understand why they don't put the passengers on another plane,' Daniel irritably said. 'But they never do, do they? I suppose they never have a spare plane in the right place, and these airlines don't give a damn about passengers being stranded for hours.' He got up. 'Well, there's no point in sitting around here when we have no idea when she'll arrive. It's a lovely evening, perfect weather for a walk beside the river. We could wander along to Barbary Wharf and have dinner as planned?'

They left five minutes later, and were just getting into the lift when they heard the phone ringing inside the flat. Daniel ran back, hurriedly hunting through his pockets for his key. He found it at last, let himself back in and ran to the phone, but it stopped ringing as he reached it.

Irena had come back, too, and looked at his frowning face with concern. 'Maybe we had better not go out, after all? Shouldn't we stay by the phone, in case that was Roz and she tries again later?'

Daniel grimaced. 'We have an answering machine. If it was working we could leave it on to record Roz's message, but it went on the blink yesterday and, typically, the engineers haven't turned up to fix it yet. I wouldn't mind, but the damned thing is state-of-the-art, it cost the earth. I got a lot of the cost on expenses because I need it for my job. It's so ultra-modern it practically cooks your dinner as well as everything else it can do—if it is working at all!'

Irena smiled. '"O brave new world..."' she quoted, and Daniel gave her an amused look.

'Oh, you know your Shakespeare, do you? That will help you with the *Sentinel*'s famous crossword puzzles. They have one every day, and fiendishly difficult they are, too. You have to have a tortuous mind. Naturally, Nick Caspian can do them, so I'm reliably informed, in the time it takes to eat his breakfast in the morning, and he does not linger over his meals!'

She laughed. 'He's frightening, isn't he? But exciting. Is it true he is in love with Christa Nordstrom?'

Daniel shrugged. 'Who knows? He isn't the type to kiss and tell, and I'm not one of her personal friends.' He and Irena left the flat once more and this time the telephone did not summon them back.

Irena had changed into a delicate pink and grey chiffon dress which gave the appearance of being floating veils clinging to her as she walked. Over that, she had slipped a little angora jacket sewn with tiny pearls here and there.

It was a warm, calm evening, the river shimmering softly in the fading sunlight, windows in office blocks were showing yellow as lights were turned on, great flocks of starlings were going home to roost on London trees and buildings, their noise deafening before they settled down to go to sleep, and there was an occasional rustle, a low whisper, from the leaves on the trees lining the new embankment gardens below the Barbary Wharf complex.

Daniel and Irena did not hurry; they strolled along, Daniel pointing out places of interest. As evening fell, the outlines of buildings showed up more on the skyline, St Paul's and Big Ben looking like cardboard cut-outs with the setting sun behind them.

They finally walked up into the Plaza gardens which lay in the heart of Barbary Wharf and which, in the evenings, were lit by Victorian-style globe-lamps which shed a golden glow on to the great open square.

The French restaurant, Pierre's, had an elegant green and gold striped awning above the plate-glass window through which one could see a few early diners at the candle-lit tables.

'We have a reservation, but the third person in our party has been delayed, so there are just two of us,' Daniel told the head waiter as he greeted them.

'*Pas de problème, Monsieur Bruneille,*' he murmured. 'I have given you your favourite table, in the far corner.'

As they followed him through the small bar which led into the restaurant Irena felt people watching them. Daniel nodded to a few people, spoke to one or two others, including a ravishing blonde, who had given Irena a quick, startled look. If she had been going to ask any questions she was too late. Daniel smilingly propelled Irena on towards their table without another word.

Valerie Knight stared after them, her brows lifted. Now what was Daniel Bruneille up to, dating a girl of that age when he had only just moved in with Roz Amery? Men! You couldn't trust them further than you could throw them. She had really believed Daniel was serious about Roz, but presumably he hadn't been able to resist a classy little item like that one, especially as she couldn't be more than twenty years old. Daniel was coming up to thirty-five, wasn't he? Or was he more than that? Hard to tell with some men, and he was in such good shape. He was ripe to fall for a girl nearly half his own age, anyway. Poor Roz, thought Valerie. Does she know about this other girl?

It was a Friday, the weekend had started, and Valerie was tired; she had had a busy week including some very late nights. There were shadows under her violet-blue eyes. The features department in which she worked had just lost two reporters, which meant that everyone left had far more work to do. It was the same in every department, of course. For the past six months there had been constant upheavals on the newspaper. The old management had gone, they were not part of the Caspian group, and Nick Caspian was trimming the entire staff down. The atmosphere was so edgy lately that many old *Sentinel* staff had either retired or gone of their own accord to other jobs.

It was all very disorientating, Valerie thought, as she sipped her glass of kir, the mixture of white wine and blackcurrant which made such a delicious aperitif on a summer evening. She was supposed to be having dinner with Esteban, but he hadn't arrived yet. Not that she minded waiting; she was too tired to care much about anything at that moment, so she leaned back against the velvet-covered bar seat, and closed her eyes.

'Working hard?'

The sarcastic voice wrecked her drowsy mood and she reluctantly lifted heavy lids although she didn't need to look at him to know it was Gilbey Collingwood.

'Stop it before you start!' she told him.

'Stop what?' he asked, pretending not to know.

'Getting at me!'

The back of Valerie's neck was already prickling at the way he watched her, his greeny-hazel eyes wandering from the dip of her low-cut black bodice to the long, slim legs her very short skirt left exposed. The dress was made of wild silk, an exclusive designer item she had bought second-hand from a shop specialising in designer fashions at cut prices. It was exciting, and made her look great, and she knew it. 'And stop staring!' she added crossly, though, because there was something in Gib's stare that put her nerves on edge.

'If you didn't want men to stare you wouldn't wear clothes like that!' Gib drawled, his mouth twisting.

'Not you,' Valerie snapped. 'I don't want you staring. I don't like the way you do it, practically undressing me!'

'Any time you say the word, baby,' Gib promised, and her body stiffened.

'Don't hold your breath! I never will!' He had ruined her peaceful moment—she was like a cat on hot bricks now. She would have left, if she weren't waiting for Esteban. Where was he? she thought impatiently.

'Waiting for someone?' Gib drawled.

'Go away.' She wasn't even looking at him again, she was going to ignore him.

That wasn't easy. He had a physical presence which made you notice him—he was a natural athlete who made sure of staying fit by playing hard games of rugger and squash at weekends as well as swimming, running and weight training every day. Over six feet, he had broad shoulders, a deep chest, slim hips and long legs. Valerie couldn't deny she found him attractive; he was her idea of the really sexy guy. A pity he was married.

It was Valerie's one unbreakable rule. She never dated married men. When she was eighteen she had been badly hurt through getting involved with a man who turned out to be married, and she had sworn never to let that happen to her again. Her decision had been reinforced, from time to time, by one or other of her friends, who had been reckless enough to get into an affair with a married man. After wasting months or even years of their lives, sooner or later they had realised they were never going to leave their wives and families, and they were just making fools of themselves in believing they ever would.

Gib sat down on the velvet bar seat beside her, his long thigh touching hers for a moment until she moved, giving him a cold look as she did so.

'Would it be too much to ask you to sit somewhere else? I'm meeting someone any minute, and I don't want him to get the wrong idea when he sees you.'

His only response to that was to grin mockingly. One of the reporters from the business section of the *Sentinel*, where Gib himself worked, as a stock-market analyst, walked past them on his way out, and said hello to Gib, smiling at Valerie politely too.

'Going to this party on Saturday?' he asked Gib, who nodded.

'Sure, see you there, Walter.' When the man had gone, Gib looked at Valerie sideways, crossing his long legs and leaning back, one arm snaking along the back of the seat. 'Are you going to the party?'

'Probably,' Valerie shrugged.

'Want a lift?'

She gave him a dry, ironic look. 'No, thank you.'

'Somebody else taking you?'

'Maybe.'

'Esteban?'

She gave another light shrug, and didn't bother to answer. Gib watched her sideways, and she pretended not to be aware of that, her profile rigid.

'Is he your date tonight?' Gib persisted and she nodded again. There was a silence. Valerie sipped her kir, her mouth oddly dry, as if with nerves.

She hated to admit it, but Gib Collingwood did get on her nerves. He annoyed her, too. Why couldn't he take no for an answer and leave her alone?

'My lawyer tells me my divorce should be heard any day now!' he suddenly said.

'So you keep telling me,' Valerie snapped. 'But it never seems to happen.'

'These things take time! My lawyer tells me there's a log jam of cases waiting to be heard, and I'll just have to be patient.' He turned right round and looked into her face. 'My wife is living with another man and expecting his baby, Valerie. She wants a divorce as desperately as I do.'

'Sure,' she said cynically.

'Look, what can I do to prove I'm telling you the truth? I'd give you her address and tell you to go and see her, but she's on the other side of the world.'

Valerie gave him a dry smile. 'Of course, she would be.'

Gib sat in silence for a few moments, glowering at her averted profile, then said, 'Last month, I was at a CI conference...'

'Which conference?' She tried to remember which organisation had those initials and Gib gave her a wry glance.

'Caspian International.'

'Oh,' she said, then laughed. 'Of course. Stupid of me to forget. I suppose I still haven't acclimatised to being part of the Caspian group. I still think the paper belongs to the Tyrrells.'

'Then you had better forget them fast, because with every week that goes by the name Tyrrell fades a little bit more, and Nick Caspian tightens his grip on the *Sentinel*,' Gib said with a grim little smile, and she shivered.

'You make it sound . . . frightening . . .'

'I saw a lot of him in Luxembourg City at this conference, and he is frightening,' Gib nodded. 'But, as I was saying, while I was there I also met an accountant who works in the Madrid paper.'

Valerie stiffened, immediately alert.

'He knew Esteban Sebastian quite well,' Gib softly said. 'He went to his wedding.'

Valerie's eyes turned a deep angry violet. 'That's a lie! Esteban isn't married. I've been to his flat and there's no sign of a woman living there.'

Coldly, Gib said, 'He may not have her with him in London, but he's a married man. Don't take my word for it——'

'I won't!' she began, but he raised his voice over hers. 'Ask him! Just ask him.'

He got up and walked away into the restaurant. Valerie threw a furious stare after him and couldn't help noticing several women turning to look after him, too, admiring the easy stride, the straight back and the supple body moving under his smoothly tailored business suit. Gib might chase her from time to time, but he was chased in his turn, and Valerie in all honesty couldn't deny that if he hadn't been married . . .

Well, he was! she told herself crossly. And how could he lie about Esteban that way? He had been sniping away at her over Esteban for ages, but she hadn't thought he would actually lie about him! Because it was a lie! She knew it couldn't be true, because she had asked Esteban when they first met, 'I suppose you've got a wife back home?', laughing up at him, half expecting him to nod, but he had shaken his head with that serious, even sombre expression which often fell over his tanned face and said quietly, 'No, I have nobody waiting for me anywhere.'

They had still been strangers then, but it hadn't entered her head to doubt his words—and now that she knew Esteban better she was absolutely certain he had told her the truth. Esteban's deeply ingrained sense of his own dignity wouldn't allow him to lie, especially about something so important, and, anyway, there had been a sadness in his voice, a loneliness that had been totally convincing.

Not that Esteban had told her much about himself, even now. He was not a talkative man. In fact he was reticent, almost never volunteered information about his previous life, and, if she asked questions, answered softly, after considerable thought. It wouldn't amaze her to find that there was much about him she did not know—but she was certain he was a man of integrity, all the same.

It was Esteban's serious nature, his dark, unsmiling features, that had attracted her in the first place: he was her absolute opposite, and there was no doubt about it, she thought, half-smiling: opposites attracted!

She heard the door from the Plaza swing open and looked towards it. Esteban came towards her, in long strides. 'I am so sorry, Valerie,' he said in his deep voice, sounding very grave, very Spanish. 'I was held up by this terrible news about Roz Amery.'

'What terrible news about Roz?' asked Valerie, frowning.

Esteban sat down beside her and took one of her hands, stroking it gently. 'You haven't heard? I'm sorry, is she a friend of yours? She was coming back from Rome when her plane was hijacked by terrorists.'

'Oh, my God!' Valerie's violet eyes opened to their fullest. 'How terrible. Is she OK? I mean, she isn't... I mean, is there any news of her?'

'Not yet, except that she's definitely on the plane.'

Valerie shivered. 'I could never be a foreign correspondent. My nerves would never stand it. Poor Roz, it's dreadful news—have they told her father?' Then, suddenly, she remembered Daniel, and turned her head to stare across the bar into the shadowy restaurant. 'Daniel can't know yet,' she thought aloud, remembering his smiling face as he walked past. There had been no shadow on it, no fear, or distress.

'We can't find him,' said Esteban, sounding terse, almost angry.

'He's here,' she said. 'In the corner, over there...'

Esteban followed her pointing hand, made a harsh, wordless sound which was not at all English, and stood up. 'Will you please to excuse me for a moment, Valerie? I am going to speak to him.'

Valerie got to her feet, too, but Esteban turned glittering dark eyes on her, made a peremptory gesture. 'No, please, stay here.'

He turned on his heel and strode away and she stared after him, open-mouthed. Very masterful! she thought, half amused, half irritated. He found it easy to give orders, didn't he? It came naturally to him. What sort of family did he come from in Spain? She could just imagine him in a bull-ring, facing life and death under a hot Spanish sun—and then she broke off the picture, laughing at herself. What nonsense!

Daniel and Irena were completely unaware of the tall, black-haired man bearing down on them. They were too absorbed in each other. Daniel was telling Irena a complicated and hilarious anecdote about her father, and she was laughing as she listened, delighted to hear anything about Des, to add to her tiny store of knowledge about him, leaning her elbows on the table, her chin in her cupped hands. Her long pale hair fell over one shoulder; she looked very young, and very beautiful, her enormous grey eyes shimmering mysteriously in her delicate face.

Esteban watched her as he walked towards her, and his dark face hardened. To him it looked as if this young girl was madly in love with the man sitting opposite her, and that made him angrier. He halted beside the table and Daniel looked up at him with a start of surprise.

'Oh, hello, Esteban.' He smiled in a friendly way. 'You again? We keep bumping into each other, don't we?'

Esteban didn't smile back. He just said curtly, 'I have bad news for you, I'm afraid. I know Nick Caspian wanted to break it to you himself. Everyone has been hunting high and low for you, ringing your flat, trying to track you down through your friends, but nobody knew where you were.'

Daniel caught the grim note in his voice, or perhaps at the back of his mind he had been intuitively anxious all evening. He stiffened in his chair, staring fixedly at the other man. 'What news? What are you talking about?'

Irena looked at him in anxious sympathy, and put her small, pale hand on top of his, as it clenched on the table.

Esteban saw the gesture, and his black brows snapped together. 'While you've been dating your new girlfriend, Roz has been sitting it out in Cyprus in a hijacked plane,' he bit out contemptuously.

Daniel turned to stone.

Irena hadn't been able to follow what Esteban said. Her English had deserted her, or else the Spaniard's thick accent had made his English too difficult for her, especially when he delivered the words so angrily. He was a very disturbing man—why was he staring at them like that, as if they had done something very wrong?

'What does he mean?' she asked Daniel frowningly. 'Sitting it out in a plane where?' As she began to work out the sense of what Esteban had snapped at them, she went white. 'Daniel! Has something bad happened to Roz?'

Daniel didn't answer. He was grey, haggard, beads of sweat on his forehead, and he began to talk jerkily, hoarsely. 'When did this happen? Hijacked? Terrorists? Who? Was anyone hurt? Did you say Cyprus? How the hell did her plane get there, starting out from Rome?'

'Terrorists?' repeated Irena, understanding the word. 'Daniel, what has happened to my sister?'

Esteban's head swung, his eyes narrowed and sharp. 'Sister? Roz is your sister?' He searched her face for some resemblance and found none, almost wondered if he had misunderstood what she said.

'Tell me, for God's sake!' snarled Daniel, on his feet now. 'Is Roz alive?'

Everyone else in the restaurant was listening to them, whispering to each other, faces shocked because they all worked on the *Sentinel* and they all knew Daniel and Esteban, and most of them knew Roz Amery, too.

'We don't know,' Esteban said slowly, still staring at Irena, and frowning.

Daniel turned on his heel and walked fast towards the door. 'I have to go,' he told the head waiter, who had been alerted by what looked like the beginning of a nasty scene and was hovering around to try to save the situation if he could. 'Send the bill to my office, will you?'

The man bowed. 'Certainly, Monsieur Bruneille.'

Irena caught up with Daniel outside in the Plaza, catching hold of his arm. The sun had set and the Victorian globes glowed dangerously against the dark night sky.

'Where are you going? Daniel, what has happened to Roz? I don't understand, please, tell me...'

'Her plane has been forced to fly to Cyprus by terrorists,' Daniel said flatly.

'Oh, no...' she whispered, her eyes dark in a white face, and he looked down at her and sighed because she was so young, but he had no time to soothe her terror.

'Look, Irena, I have to go now, I'm in a hurry to get to Roz as soon as I can—I have to be there, on the spot, you understand? In case...'

She gripped his hand, nodding. 'For when they let her go,' she quickly said. 'She'll need you.'

His mouth quivered, bloodless. 'Yes. I'm sorry to have to leave you alone. I'll ask Gina to look after you. You remember Gina from Paris? Here is a key to our flat, I'll get Gina to take you back there, but you just stay put and wait for news.'

He turned without waiting for her to reply, and began to run across the Plaza and Irena followed, clutching the key he had given her in her trembling hand. Before they had gone far, they met Nick Caspian and Gina coming to find them, having had a phone call from Esteban to say that Daniel was on his way.

Daniel stopped dead in his tracks, waiting for them to join him. Gina put her arms round him and hugged him, tears in her eyes.

'Oh, Daniel . . .'

He stared at Nick's grim face over her shoulder. 'Any more news?' he hoarsely demanded.

'I'm afraid so,' Nick said, and Daniel could see in the other man's eyes that he was wondering how to break whatever news he had to tell.

Fiercely, Daniel said, 'Just give it to me, Nick. Don't wrap it up.'

Nick sighed. 'The terrorists have set a deadline. Either their demands are met by noon tomorrow, or they'll start shooting the hostages, one every hour.'

# CHAPTER THREE

GINA said to Daniel quietly, 'Don't you think it would be better if Irena came home with me? You know what some reporters can be like—one of our rival papers might send somebody along to your flat, and you wouldn't want Irena to be on the receiving end of media attention, would you?'

'No, you're right,' Daniel agreed, with only half his mind on what she was saying because he was thinking about Roz and sweating. He couldn't rest, couldn't think clearly, he could only think about Roz. 'Thanks for the offer, Gina.'

'So if you ring, remember, she's at my place,' Gina said, watching him, aware that he was not really listening, and understanding.

'I'll remind him when he rings me from Cyprus,' Nick muttered to her, turning his dark head and leaning down towards her, so that Daniel shouldn't hear.

Irena hugged Daniel, tears in her eyes. She tried to say something comforting, but her English broke down before the force of her emotion.

He patted her shoulder roughly. 'It will be OK, Irena. You're not to worry about Roz. She's been in tight spots before, she has her head screwed on. Gina will look after you—she lives in the same apartment block as we do.' Over her head he gave Gina a pleading look and Gina stepped forward to put an arm around Irena.

'We had better go now,' she gently said. 'Daniel and the others have a lot to do.'

47

Irena nodded and walked away with just one brief, backward look at Daniel's drawn face, wishing she could go with him. Gina drove her back to the apartment block, Irena went into Daniel's flat to collect a few things for the night, and then they both went up to Gina's penthouse flat. To Irena the lift seemed to go up and up, but it could only have been a few more floors because the block was not a skyscraper. To reach the top floor, even if you lived in the building, you needed a special security key, both for the lift and for the stairs.

'Nobody can just drop in!' Gina said lightly. 'They have to ring from Reception, and the porter brings them up.'

There were only two flats on the top floor, Gina told her, and the other one belonged to the man who had built the block, but lived in the Cayman Islands most of the year.

'I've never even seen him,' Gina smiled, showing Irena round her own flat. 'This is the sitting-room.'

'It is very elegant,' Irena said politely, forcing a smile which almost hurt her. It was true, the room was exquisitely furnished, but she had to make herself show an interest she could not feel at that moment.

She looked at the television set in the corner, half afraid, half longing to turn it on for the latest news.

'I didn't furnish it,' Gina said wryly. 'I inherited everything in this room, from my husband's grandfather, and there seemed no point in buying any new furniture of my own. Having familiar stuff around me makes the flat seem more like home.'

'Your husband's grandfather...' Irena thought aloud, remembering all that Des had told her. 'That was Sir George...'

Gina nodded. 'Tyrrell. Yes, Sir George Tyrrell. I wish you had known him—he was a darling, and I loved him very much.'

Irena tore her eyes from the TV set and looked around her. 'You live here alone?' She suddenly realised just how spacious and luxurious the apartment was—why, she thought, the sitting-room was bigger than the whole of Des's Paris apartment.

Gina gave her a rueful smile. 'I know, it's much too big for one person—but you should have seen the house I lived in before I moved here! The old man left me his home, too—I hated selling it because I know he loved the house, but it was a small palace, much too big for one person.'

'Do you do your own housework?' Irena uncertainly asked, noticing that the furniture was antique, and obviously valuable—brocade-covered eighteenth-century chairs and sofas, highly polished tables and chests, delicate porcelain and glass, a gold-framed mirror on one wall, paintings hanging on the other. The room was immaculate, not a speck of dust to be seen, nothing out of place. Somebody worked very hard to keep it looking like that.

Gina shook her head. 'Someone comes in every weekday morning, but with only me living here the place never gets really untidy, so there isn't that much to do. Come and see your bedroom.'

Irena looked at the TV and opened her mouth to protest, but Gina was already walking out of the room, so Irena sighed and followed her into a pretty pink and cream bedroom. 'It is lovely,' she said huskily.

But she wasn't looking at the décor or the furniture— she was staring at the small white television on a table opposite the bed.

Gina smiled. 'Good, well, you settle in here while I make some hot chocolate for us both. I think you should get to bed early, don't you? You've had a very tiring day.' She had carried Irena's overnight bag along the corridor; she put it on the end of the bed and Irena smiled back with an effort, her mouth quivering and her enormous grey eyes bleak.

Gina went out, closing the door behind her, and Irena rushed to switch on the TV set and then impatiently flicked from channel to channel until she found a news programme. She stood listening, biting her thumb-nail like a child, staring fixedly at the screen. There was the aircraft, filmed from far away, looking like a toy; but this was not a game, it was deadly serious.

There was no real news. The plane had landed in Cyprus, the local police were talking to the terrorists on the plane's radio, nothing was happening. Nobody had been shot yet, and to Irena that was all that mattered. She sighed in relief then, leaving the screen switched on, unpacked like an automaton—laid out her nightdress on the bed, hung up her dressing-gown in the wardrobe, her mind restlessly busy with thoughts of her half-sister.

Gina meant well, but Irena knew she would never sleep tonight, not knowing whether Roz was alive or dead. It seemed like a grim joke on the part of fate that she should find out after all these years that she had a half-sister, only to be faced with losing her so soon afterwards, and in such a terrifying fashion.

She drew back the curtains to look out over night-time London; the dazzling lights from the buildings on the skyline, the gleam of reflections on the dark water of the river, made it look like a carnival or a party, which grated on her distracted, anxious mood.

She wished she were back in Spain, standing in her own room in the little farmhouse, looking out over darkness and silence, no lights of any other house in view, only the icy glitter of the stars above in the deep, night sky and the black curve of the mountains rolling across the horizon. For the first time for ages, she was homesick; she felt lost, out of place, alien here. She closed her eyes and thought of home, and imagined being back there.

It would be so still; now and then a wail from one of the wild cats who lived around the barns, and kept down rats and mice. Or the sigh of the wind in the olive trees, a dog barking down in the valley, the rustle of the orange trees planted in great, straw-wrapped terracotta pots along one wall of the farmhouse, to catch the sun.

The farm lay inland, fifty miles from the coastal strip with its white hotels and tropical gardens, its blocks and apartments for foreigners, its restaurants and night-clubs. That was a Spain Irena did not know. She had grown up in a much older Spain: one whose soil had been soaked in blood during the bitter civil war, one which had known hunger and death; bitter cold and fierce wind in winter, the savagery of the sun in summer. Life was not easy in those stark, barren hills; they still had not caught up with the modern conveniences of life as it was lived down on the coast; their electricity broke down when the wind brought down power lines, there was no refuse collection or sewage pipes. In many ways they lived as their ancestors had done, but she loved her home, she yearned to be back there.

London was strange and frightening. It had a threat-ening look tonight; the sulphurous amber glow from street lights reflected on the heavy clouds, the black bulk of towering blocks looming on the horizon. Even the permanent sound of traffic sounded like the roar of an angry lion.

She wished she could go to Des for comfort, and comfort him in turn, but he was on his way to Vietnam by now, and there was no way of reaching him on the plane—he would only find out what was happening to his daughter when he arrived, no doubt. Irena ached for him. This would hit him hard; he would feel it far more than even she did because he had known Roz all her life whereas Irena had not yet had a real chance to get to know her half-sister.

There had been a time when Irena had been bitter towards Des—but that had been before she met him and felt the instant tug of a feeling she had not anticipated. She had liked Des on sight. Now, she loved him, and she had been through much the same process with Roz. When she first heard about her, she had been jealous because Roz had always been with Des; they were obviously very close, Des mentioned her all the time. Irena had felt shut out, excluded from the small family unit they made. Then she had met Roz at last, and been touched and moved beyond words when Roz at once greeted her as a sister, showed no sign of holding back or being hostile.

This visit to London was to have been her chance to get to know Roz properly, but now she might never have that chance. Irena felt her eyes burn with unshed tears.

'The chocolate is ready!' said Gina quietly behind her. Irena hadn't even heard her open the door.

'I'm coming,' she muttered, rubbing a hand across her eyes.

'If you're going to watch TV you might as well watch it with me,' Gina said on a sigh. 'Come on... although I don't suppose there will be any news for ages.'

* * *

In Cyprus, the plane had landed and taxied to the centre of the runway, where it came to a halt. It was night-time now, but the great arc lights lit up the whole airport in an eerie way, like sheet lightning.

If she looked sideways Roz could see the perimeter: police and military vehicles parked at a safe distance, men with binoculars watching the plane, the glitter of the lights on the barrels of rifles and machine-guns. Now and then someone darted from cover then ran back into it again. One man in a white shirt and dark trousers stood in the open for a moment, studying the plane through his binoculars.

How much could he see? Was he watching her while she watched him? At a distance, he could have been Daniel: tall, thin, black-haired. There was a blurred dazzle in her eyes; she shut them and blinked rapidly. She was not going to cry. She straightened her back, lifted her chin, stared straight ahead.

A woman in front of her was cuddling a crying child, murmuring comfortingly. The youngest of the gunmen shouted at her to make the child be quiet, and she flinched, bending over her little girl, putting a hand over her mouth, whispering urgently to her in Italian, and the child sniffled and hid her face against her mother.

The gunman who spoke English came out from the cockpit and muttered to his two companions in what Roz thought was Arabic; she wished she had learnt more of the language. The trouble was that in those Arab countries she had visited with her father she had found it easy to get by with French, which was usually spoken in places like Algeria or Morocco which had at some time been under French rule.

Suddenly, the terrorist leader barked an order. 'Get out your passports!'

Everyone stirred, pale faces tense, relieved to be allowed to move, to do something, yet wondering what the order might mean, whether there was some chance that they might be allowed to leave, or there was some more sinister motive behind the command. Roz had her passport in her handbag; she found it quickly and held it, feeling the sweat trickling down her back, making her shirt stick to her, making her face glisten wetly.

The gunman pointed at a suntanned young boy in jeans and a T-shirt. 'You! Collect the passports and bring them to me.'

While the gunmen watched, their weapons pointed at his back, the boy walked shakily down the aisle to collect the passports. Roz gave him a sympathetic look as she handed hers over: he was barely fifteen, very pale under his summer tan. He had probably been on holiday in Italy, had been on his way home; he was alone, and his parents must be frantic.

Daniel must be out of his mind, too. She closed her eyes. She would not think about Daniel. It would only make her cry. But how did she stop? Her mind kept throwing up thoughts about him.

She might never see Daniel again. Never. The word tolled in her head and she shivered. Never. What a terrifying word.

The terrorist leader took the passports and walked away with them, into the cockpit of the plane. Outside, the passengers heard the wail of sirens, the screech of tyres on tarmac, and they stirred, whispering to each other.

'Silence. Keep still. No talking.' Screaming orders, the two gunmen moved sideways, like crabs, to the windows, watching the passengers, their weapons trained on them, then one of them looked out while the other kept his eyes on the passengers. The activity outside the plane was all at a distance, nobody was approaching the plane, and the terrorists relaxed again, but Roz could see that they were both shaking.

They are as scared as we are, she thought, and they have as much chance of ending up dead. That young one—how old is he? Eighteen? Twenty? He had the smooth skin of a child, his features almost female in their beauty. The other was pock-marked, gaunt, with burning, angry black eyes, and he was on a hair-trigger. Anything might make him explode. But he wasn't the one that really frightened Roz—it was the older man, the leader. His eyes were icy with hate. He was capable of anything.

The minutes dragged by, and became hours, her head slid sideways and her eyelids drooped. She slept fitfully and began to dream of being on a plane and being hi-jacked. A man with eyes full of hate turned a gun on her, her heart raced and her body was drenched with perspiration, she screamed.

With a violent jerk she woke up. She opened her eyes and at once was aware that her dream had been real. Her heart still thudding, her mouth dry, she stared around the plane, dazed and red-eyed. Others were asleep; leaning on each other, slumped in their seats. She saw another woman wake up with the same sudden physical jolt she had felt herself, saw the woman's face, her terrified eyes, her start as she looked about her, and knew that the other had dreamt the same dream and woken to find it was not a dream.

Roz shifted in her seat and almost screamed out. She had cramp, her muscles tortured after hours of staying in one position, especially in that temperature.

She looked out of the window and saw dawn in the distance, streaking the sky with fire. Another hot day ahead, with the sun beating down on the metal fuselage of the plane, turning it into an oven! During the night the temperature had dropped slightly, but as the day wore on it was going to be unbearably hot inside this plane. She was hot enough now.

She thought of water with intense yearning. Her mouth was parched and hot and tasted foul. Her clothes stuck to her and her head throbbed. Some of the children were grizzling quietly; they must be thirsty, too, and terrified, and it must be harder for them to stay still for so long.

Roz watched the darkness slowly melting away, the sunrise spreading. The beauty of that sky was breathtaking; it brought tears to the eyes. She had never seen anything so lovely and she didn't know why she should cry over it, but all her reactions seemed more intense than they had ever been in her life before. Maybe that was what people meant when they talked about the possibility of death concentrating the mind? A wry smile twisted her mouth and at that instant she met the eyes of the terrorist leader, and her smile died.

Irena slept through the dawn. She and Gina had stayed up until the early hours, watching TV until it closed down, and then Gina had insisted that they both went to bed.

'It won't do Roz any good if you make yourself ill! And I don't suppose for a minute that anything will happen overnight; these hijack situations seem to drag on and on for hours. But if there is any news I'm sure we'll hear at once—Daniel will ring us from Cyprus, he knows my number.'

Irena had been so tired that she hadn't argued much. She had stumbled back to the pink and cream bedroom, fallen into bed and lain awake with jumping nerves until she drifted at last into sleep. She had dreams, too, and they strangely echoed Roz's; violent and terrifying dreams from which she woke briefly, several times, before falling into a much deeper sleep which was not broken by nightmares.

When she woke up next time it was mid-morning and already hot. Irena had kicked off all the covers and for an instant she thought she was back in Spain, on the farm. She felt happy and smiled, and then her memory came back and she jerked upwards, immediately on edge and trembling.

Roz. What time was it? She looked at her watch. Twenty past eleven! Gina had let her sleep for hours! Anything could have happened to Roz while she slept. She leapt off the bed and as she did someone tapped on the door.

Irena's nerves leapt. 'What is it?' she whispered in Spanish, and there was silence outside, then Gina's voice said uncertainly,

'Irena? Are you awake?'

'Yes, what has happened?' Irena said in English, and opened the door.

Gina was fully dressed, but rather pale. 'Nothing,' she said quickly. 'There is no news yet, no real news, nothing has happened.' She looked into Irena's anxious eyes and added, 'Nobody has been shot, the terrorists are negotiating, they've asked for food and drink and medicines.'

Irena gave a shaky sigh of relief.

'I brought you some coffee,' Gina said, offering her a mug. 'I thought I heard you moving about.'

'How long have you been up?'

'Not long. An hour, maybe.'

'Why didn't you wake me? You should have woken me.' Anger made her voice shake and Gina looked at her anxiously.

'Oh, but Irena...you needed sleep, you had a bad day yesterday and you didn't go to bed until gone three. I thought I should let you sleep as long as you could. I'm sorry if you're upset, but I did it for the best.'

Irena grimaced, sighing. 'I am sorry, Gina. I shouldn't have snapped at you, I'm just so worried about Roz.'

'I know, and if there had been any news I'd have woken you at once, but as there wasn't I thought it would be best if you caught up on your sleep. You feel better, don't you? Good, then enjoy your coffee, have a shower, get dressed and we'll have something to eat.'

'I don't want anything,' Irena said, shaking her head, but Gina gave her a firm look.

'You must eat something, or you'll make yourself ill. A little salad, some fruit...it will help to pass the time while we wait for news.'

'Are you always this bossy?' Irena asked with a rueful little smile, and Gina laughed.

'Only for your own good!'

She went back to the kitchen and began making a light meal, midway between breakfast and lunch—salad and fruit with a little smoked salmon which she would serve with hot scrambled eggs, she decided. She heard the shower running a little while later and knew that Irena wouldn't be long.

The phone rang and she leapt to answer it, but it was only Philip calling to ask her out to lunch.

'I'd have loved to, but I've got Roz's sister staying with me and I can't leave her here alone,' Gina said.

'Why not? How old is she?'

'Irena's about twenty, but at the moment, with Roz in this hijacked plane, she's very worried, and I don't think she should be left alone.'

Philip was sulky. 'What a nuisance! I'll have to have lunch alone, then, and I hate eating alone.'

'Come here and eat with us!' she coaxed, half smiling, half sighing, because he could be very childish when he was crossed.

'No,' he said sullenly, 'I'd find it depressing to have Roz Amery's little sister weeping all over the place.'

As Gina put the phone down Irena hurried into the room, her hair still damp from the shower. 'Was that news of Roz?' she eagerly asked, and Gina shook her head.

'A friend of mine. How are you feeling now?'

'Better.'

'Well, come and eat,' Gina said. 'It's almost midday now and I am starving, I don't know about you. I'll just microwave these eggs to go with the smoked salmon.'

Irena was not hungry, but the beautifully presented fruit and salad looked so deliciously refreshing that she found herself eating more than she had expected, including some smoked salmon and scrambled eggs with a surprising salad of pineapple, peach, strawberries and a tossed green salad of mixed lettuces, cucumber, avocado and endive. With it she drank mixed fruit juices which Gina had freshly squeezed and chilled in the fridge for an hour, and then they drank their coffee while they watched the one o'clock news.

Nothing much seemed to have happened except that the terrorists had been supplied with everything they demanded: medicines and food and fresh water.

The news ended, they switched to other channels but there was no further information to be got anywhere, so they turned off the set and Irena gave a long sigh.

'Oh, how much longer will it go on?'

'It could be days,' Gina said, watching her with sympathy and compassion. 'We just have to be patient.'

'I know, but it is hard—if only Daniel would ring!'

'I'm sure he will, soon,' said Gina. 'He must be there by now.'

Indeed, Nick's private jet had already landed on a small private airfield some three-quarters of an hour from Nicosia. A chauffeur-driven car had met Daniel there. While the plane was on its way to Cyprus, Hazel had been very busy on the phone making all the necessary arrangements to expedite Daniel's journey from one airport to the other. Daniel was rushed into the back of the black limousine, and whisked away at speed.

'I get you there soon! Very good driver. I do funerals, do funerals,' shouted the uniformed driver to him. 'I give you my card, in case you ever need me.'

Daniel was speechless as he listened to the driver's sales talk all the way to the airport where the hijacked plane stood isolated in the middle of the empty tarmac. The first sight that met Daniel's eyes was not the plane, however. It was the mass of vehicles on the perimeter: ambulances, fire engines, cars, police vans, military trucks and jeeps.

As Daniel stumbled out of the car, police surrounded him and insisted on searching him systematically, from head to foot, studying his passport and other identity papers.

Then one man drew him aside, hard black eyes assessing Daniel's face. Daniel looked at the other's uniform. An army officer, he recognised; and a high-ranking one, at that, in his late forties, very fit, very bronzed, with a face like a stone wall.

'We were told that you were on your way, Mr Bruneille,' he said through his teeth, without warmth.

Daniel could imagine the string-pulling Nick Caspian had been doing, and if he had not been so worried he might have smiled. The army officer clearly did not like having to be polite to him, yet had been given his orders from above.

'I'm sorry,' the man said without meaning a word of it. 'But I have a job to do, and I cannot let you interfere with that. I must ask you to join the Press corps in the airport building, and stay with them. If you were not a journalist I would ask you to leave the area altogether. We don't want relatives here; they can do nothing useful, they would only get in our way. This is a military operation; the situation out there is very volatile. It could swing the wrong way any minute, we have some tense negotiations going on and we don't have the time to wet-nurse a civilian.'

'At least tell me what is going on!' Daniel said.

'You'll be briefed inside the terminal building,' the officer said, turning away.

'Now, look——' Daniel began, and then a soldier grabbed his arm, hustling him towards a jeep.

'Stop pushing me around!' Daniel snapped.

The soldier shoved him into the jeep without answering, and started the engine.

'Will you tell me what has happened so far, then?' Daniel asked and the soldier turned indifferent eyes on him.

'No Englis!' he said triumphantly.

Daniel didn't know whether to believe him or not, but as they were driving at speed across bumpy ground he could only accept the answer.

Ben Winter, the *Sentinel* reporter from the home desk who had picked up on the hijack story simply by being in the airport when the news first broke, met Daniel as he was thrust into the room where the reporters were waiting for news.

'They told me you were on your way, Daniel, but I didn't expect you this soon!'

'Caspian sent me in his own jet.'

Ben grimaced. 'I flew here economy with my wife and kids, and it took me hours, let me tell you. I suppose you're going to take over from me?'

'If you want to get on with your holiday, I will.' Daniel shrugged.

'I'm not desperate to do that. This is a terrific story, and I did get on to it first. I ought to get my byline for this one!'

Daniel laughed shortly, eyeing him with some sympathy. 'Haven't you had a byline on your stuff before?'

'Not on the *Sentinel*, I'm just a staff reporter, but this is different, after all.'

Daniel nodded. 'I'll speak to Fabien later today. I'm sure he'll give you your byline. We could share the byline, in fact, and don't imagine I'm asking for top billing, because I've got other things on my mind.' He paused, then asked urgently, 'Any news?'

Ben hesitated. 'Nothing much, the deadline passed and they didn't shoot anyone...'

Daniel took a deep breath, trembling in a relief so fierce that it hurt.

Ben went on, 'And they've had hours of negotiations, they're asking for food and drink and medicine, and I gather the local guys are ready to agree.'

Huskily, Daniel said in an offhand, shaky tone, 'Makes sense. It eases the situation, takes some of the heat out of it, standard procedure.'

'I suppose you've covered hijackings before,' Ben said with respect.

Daniel nodded. 'They like to keep them talking, get to know them, work out what makes them tick, where their weak points are.' He gave a long sigh. 'Well, it sounds as if they aren't quite as unstable as it seemed at first. Now, tell me everything that's happened from the beginning...'

# CHAPTER FOUR

As THE afternoon wore on, Gina and Irena kept in constant touch with the *Sentinel* newsroom, but there was little definite news to be got. The authorities in Cyprus had imposed a black-out on information, they were only releasing as much as they felt absolutely necessary, claiming that their decision was forced on them by the situation and the need to restrict the information the terrorists received on the radio in the plane. They wanted the terrorists to depend upon them for any news they got.

On television, at least, you picked up some of the atmosphere on the airport runways from the colour pieces the TV news reporters gave. 'It's a hundred and ten in the shade out here this afternoon,' one man said, his flushed and perspiring face giving his words even more impact. 'It must be hell on earth inside that plane.'

Shortly after hearing this, Daniel rang. 'I'm afraid there is no news of Roz,' he told Irena. 'But the buzz here is that the negotiations for the release of women and children are going quite well, although it may take hours yet before it happens. I'll let you know the minute anything breaks. Try not to worry too much. Any news from Des?'

'Not a word, he can't have heard about it yet.'

'Or if he has he doesn't realise Roz is on the plane,' Daniel thought aloud.

Nick Caspian called from the office shortly after Daniel had rung off, and spoke to Gina. 'Did Daniel call you? He has filed some copy—he's working with the young reporter who first picked up the story in Cyprus. I talked to Daniel myself and he sounded calm enough, but he must be very tense, although the situation appears to be less dangerous than it seemed at first.'

'Who can tell from outside the plane what's going on inside it?' Gina snapped.

'Don't take it out on me, Gina!' Nick muttered. 'It isn't my fault this happened to Roz!'

'I didn't say it was!'

But Gina knew that subconsciously she did blame him, however unjustly, and it made her angrier that Nick had picked that up. It annoyed her when he read her mind like that, especially when she hadn't realised what was going on inside her head until Nick pointed it out to her! It was almost as if he knew her better than she knew herself, which was ridiculous, of course, and that made her angry too. In fact, she only had to hear his voice to feel her mental temperature rising.

'How's Irena coping?' Nick asked curtly.

'It's tough on her, but she's like Roz; she can cope with what she has to face.'

'You seem to manage it, too.'

'Women have had to,' Gina said, and he groaned.

'No women's lib stuff, please!'

Gina was so furious she had to count to ten, and then she said, 'Have you got anything else to say, Mr Caspian?'

'Go to hell,' Nick said, suddenly as angry as her. He put the phone down and Gina looked at it in some surprise. Sometimes his reactions startled her.

In the plane Roz was watching the blue sky darken towards twilight—it had been a long, exhausting, terrifying day, her body was cramped and sticky, and her head was aching so much that it made her feel quite sick. What was happening in the cockpit? she wondered, and knew that all the other passengers wondered, too, their eyes fixed on the front of the plane where the youngest of the terrorists was on guard. They all knew that negotiations had been taking place since the delivery of the food and water and medicines, but no announcement had been made as to precisely what the terrorists' demands were.

The stewardess was nursing one of the children, a small boy whose mother had fallen asleep, her head on her husband's shoulder.

Where was Daniel? Roz wondered, staring at the perimeter where lights had begun to blaze again as the light faded. Was he out there now, watching her? Des might be there, too. She knew they would both be worried and upset, but they were tougher than most men—they would be able to live with her situation far better than the average husband or father. They knew she could cope.

A sudden buzz inside the plane made her look round. All the passengers were staring at the front of the plane, as the terrorist leader returned, with a pile of passports clutched in one hand, his gun in the other. 'OK. Everybody listen! We have had long talks with the people on the ground. Some of our demands have already been met. A message is being broadcast around the world, explaining our aims and intentions...food will be distributed to the refugee camps...in return for this we have decided that all women and children are going to be allowed to leave the plane.'

There was a gasp. Faces whitened or flushed, eyes widened, women clutched at their husbands, children clung to their mothers, there was an outbreak of whispering.

'No talking!' snapped the leader. 'Stay in your seats until I tell you to move!'

He turned to confer with the other two men, a brief argument in harsh Arabic, then he turned back to face the passengers. 'Shortly, the escape chute will be released, and then one by one you will come up to the front when I call your name, and you will slide down the chute and run away from the plane without looking back. You must do exactly what you are told. If any of you disobeys in any way, we will start shooting the others still on the plane. You must follow my orders to the letter.'

Irena and Gina were watching an old Doris Day film that evening when the programme was suddenly interrupted by a newsflash.

Both girls tensed, turning pale. 'Something has happened!' Irena whispered, shaking.

Gina reached out and took hold of her hand in silence as the newsreader began to speak. As his words sank in, Irena burst into tears and Gina put her arms round her, murmuring huskily, close to tears herself, 'She's OK, don't cry...it's over...she's safe...she'll be coming home soon.'

'I can't believe it, I can't believe it,' Irena kept saying.

Gina laughed unsteadily. 'I know what you mean, but it's true, the women and children have all been released. Roz will be with Daniel now. Isn't that wonderful?'

'Wonderful,' Irena sobbed, laughing at the same time.

When she had calmed down Gina went off to make them both some hot milk and they sat drinking it in front of the lifelike electric log fire on the stone hearth which was a feature of the room. Hoping that Irena would now be able to sleep, Gina turned off most of the lights, leaving on only a table-lamp which cast a gentle pink glow.

'When we've drunk this, we'll go to bed,' she said, curling up in a corner of a sofa and yawning.

Irena sipped the milk, watching the television with the sound turned off. There was a late night programme running, music and interviews interspersed with news reports. A Tom and Jerry cartoon came on; she laughed until the tears crept down her face again, not so much because it was that funny as because her relief spilled over into easy tears and laughter; her nerves were very near the surface.

She looked across at Gina to see if she was laughing too, but Gina had fallen asleep, mouth open, head propped by the arm of the sofa. Irena suddenly saw Gina's glass of milk tilting dangerously, and leapt across to grab it from her limp hand before it dropped. Gina didn't wake up even then. Irena was just tiptoeing back to her chair when she heard a low buzz on the doorbell.

Startled, she hurried to the front door and looked through the spy hole. Nick Caspian's face loomed up at her.

She realised he was about to ring again, so she quickly took off the chain and opened the door. He was looking grey and tired, and with a little jab of shock she saw that he had Esteban Sebastian with him. Irena's lashes flickered nervously and she looked back at Nick, who, formidable though he was, somehow did not frighten her as much as the other man.

Nick said gently in Spanish, 'How are you, Irena?'

'Much happier now that I know Roz is safe!' she whispered.

'You saw that on the television news?' Nick and Esteban exchanged looks.

Irena smiled radiantly, pushing a hand through her ruffled, long pale hair. 'Yes, but please...keep your voices down. Gina is asleep, we mustn't wake her up, she is very tired. Come into the kitchen.'

She walked away and heard the two men murmuring to each other in low voices, but as she glanced back they stopped talking and followed her. Nick paused at the doorway of the softly lit sitting-room and stared at Gina, curled up like a child in the corner of the sofa, her russet-gold hair gleaming and vivid in the lamplight.

After a pause he joined Irena and Esteban in the kitchen. Irena asked, 'Can I get you something to drink? Tea or coffee?'

'Coffee, thank you,' Nick said, sitting down on a chair and crossing his long legs casually. He watched her switch on the electric coffee-making machine Gina had demonstrated to her earlier. In Paris she and Des made their coffee in the time-honoured French method; grinding their own beans in a small wooden mill, percolating them on the stove in a battered old pot which had belonged to Des's mother and with which he would not be parted. The pot itself seemed redolent of all those years of coffee-making; the flavour of every cup was rich and extraordinary. Gina's state-of-the-art machine could not match that.

'We saw you still had your light on, Irena, so we thought you might like to see a copy of the midnight edition.' Nick was carrying some copies of the paper under his arm; he dropped them on to the table and she saw the front page, a grey, grainy photo of the hijacked plane, and inset with it a smaller photo of Roz looking oddly young and boyish, with her short hair and thin face.

She picked up a copy and looked at the picture, smiling quiveringly. 'It is very thoughtful of you to do this.'

'This is a very personal story for us, Irena,' said Nick, his grey eyes kind. 'Roz is one of us—you would be surprised how many people stayed at work long after they would normally have gone home.'

Irena looked at Esteban. 'Did you write this story?'

Nick laughed. 'Esteban doesn't write for us, he's the marketing director. He's here because he was having dinner with me, and some important clients—and afterwards we went back to the *Sentinel* to pick up these copies straight from the printing shop before we came back here for a nightcap.'

'A nightcap?' she repeated, baffled by the word, and both men laughed.

'A last drink,' said Nick, and Esteban said it in Spanish, making her smile.

He had upset her when he'd shouted at her and Daniel in Pierre's restaurant, the night she'd arrived; she had been feeling disorientated already, and Esteban's hostile reaction had confused her even more, but he looked different now. His face was much warmer, kinder, less disturbing.

The coffee was ready, she set out cups, her small hands deft. 'You live in this apartment block, Mr Caspian?' Then a thought struck her. 'But how did you get up to this floor? Gina said there was a special key, for security reasons—that nobody could ever use the lift, or open the door to the stairs, unless they had a key, and there is only one other tenant on this floor, who lives in the Cayman Islands.'

'I bought the flat from him,' Nick said. 'I live there now.'

Irena gave him a quick, startled look. 'Gina knows this?'

'Not yet,' Nick said, his grey eyes gleaming with what looked remarkably like triumph. 'I must tell her.'

Would Gina be pleased when she heard? wondered Irena, but all she said was, 'She ought to be in bed. I feel guilty, keeping her up for so long, especially after last night, when we stayed up until the early hours of the morning, but I couldn't bear to wake her up to tell her to go to bed!' She smiled at the two men, and Nick and Esteban exchanged another look.

'I'll carry her to bed now,' Nick said, getting up again.

'Oh, I don't think...' began Irena in protest.

He was already halfway out of the door. She was following him when Esteban distracted her, his face and voice sombre.

'Irena, wait a minute. There's something I have to tell you.'

She looked round picking up the note in his voice, a premonition creeping over her like a shiver.

'What is it?' A hand went up to her mouth. 'It's Roz, isn't it?'

'They didn't release her,' Esteban said quietly. 'Her passport told them that she was a journalist and they decided she might be useful to them so they kept her on board.'

'Oh no...' she breathed, beginning to tremble.

Esteban put a comforting arm around her shoulders. 'At least you can be sure they won't harm her,' he quickly said. 'They obviously intend her to write the sort of story they want to see in the Press, so they'll treat her well. Knowing Roz, she will probably be quite pleased to stay on there. If she didn't enjoy danger and excitement, she would never have become a foreign correspondent. She's her father's daughter, after all. Des would have wanted to stay on that plane.'

Irena stood in silence, staring at nothing. It was true, after all—she couldn't deny it. Roz was the image of their father, in looks and nature. Irena knew she had nothing of Des in her. Not for the first time since she found him in Paris she wondered if her mother had lied— was she really Des's child? Then she remembered the photograph of Des's mother, the uncanny resemblance to herself, now, and she sighed. Yes, she was his daughter, and Roz's sister.

'I am so sorry to bring you this news,' he said in his deep voice, his hand rhythmically stroking down her long brown hair. It felt so good; Irena didn't want it to stop, she wished she could just lean on him like a child and give herself up to that stroking hand.

But she was an adult, so she said huskily, 'It was kind of you to break it so gently; I'm glad I didn't hear it on television. It would have been a terrible shock.'

Esteban stopped stroking her hair and looked down into her small face.

'You are very brave,' he said, and lifted her hand to his mouth, to kiss it, surprising her so much that she didn't move, just watched him, colour flowing up to her hairline.

Esteban's eyes, so black and glistening, like sloe-berries, gazed back at her intently. 'I spoke very harshly to you the other night, at the restaurant,' he murmured, 'And I am sorry. I completely misunderstood the situation. I like Roz very much, and I thought Daniel was betraying her, that you were his new girlfriend. I was very angry—but it was unforgivable, talking to a child like you in that way!'

'I'm not a child!' she said indignantly, and Esteban laughed, his hard face softening into amusement and warmth.

'Of course not. I am sorry again.' He gave her a dark-eyed glance, teasing a little. 'I hope I am not always going to be apologising to you!'

Nick, meanwhile, was standing beside the sofa looking down at Gina, who was in a deep sleep, her lids flickering rapidly, showing the white gleam of her eyeballs. She must be dreaming, he thought, wishing he could see inside her head. She was a mystery to him, one he would give anything to unravel. She was wearing a thin white lawn robe over a matching night-dress; both garments so fine that he could see the delicate pink glimmer of her skin through them both, and he couldn't take his eyes off her small, high breasts, the darker pink of her nipples pressing against the thin material. She had been wearing slippers which had come off, leaving her small feet bare. A dark flush crept over Nick's hard face as he watched her. She was beautiful. A wave of heat went through him and he swallowed, his throat moving convulsively.

He knelt down and softly brushed his mouth along one of her naked feet, kissed her ankle, her pale, satiny skin, her toes, then looked up at her again. Gina didn't wake up, she didn't even stir, oblivious of everything.

He stood up and bent over her, slid one arm under her and picked her up in one swift movement; her head falling back over his forearm and her body limp.

For a moment he stood there, hardly breathing, but she didn't wake up, so he walked with great slowness and care along the corridor, so as not to wake her.

He paused at the end of the corridor—now which room would most likely be hers?

Probably the biggest, since this was her flat, so he went into that and saw at once that he was right because the fitted wardrobe stood open, exposing rows and rows of clothes, some of which he recognised. Irena must be using the room next door.

He carried Gina over to her bed, which was turned down for the night, and lowered her on to it. As her body touched the cool sheets she sighed and her eyelids fluttered upwards; her drowsy green eyes looked into his face. Nick was still bent over her, one arm underneath her body. For a moment they stared at each other, and then Nick gave a stifled groan, and his mouth began searching for hers in a blind movement, his eyes almost shut.

Gina was warm and relaxed, half-asleep still, she had been dreaming about him, a dream of intense passion, and desire burned high inside her, for a second or two she almost believed she was still dreaming, and she kissed him back, her body melting in the heat that flared between them. When she was awake she might be able to subdue her deepest instincts, but when she slept her own nature betrayed her, her love for Nick overwhelmed everything else.

Nick came down on to the bed beside her, kissing her with a hunger that matched her own, murmuring passionately, 'Gina. Oh, Gina...'

The sound of his voice snapped her out of her tranced state like a smack around the face. Her green eyes opened fully, dark with shock, her body stiffened. This was no dream. This was really happening, Nick was here, in her bedroom, lying on her bed with her—but how?

She remembered watching television with Irena, remembered getting drowsier, falling asleep on the sofa in the sitting-room, but how had she got to her bedroom—and where had Nick sprung from?

Nick was oblivious, quite unaware of the change in Gina; too absorbed in his own needs and feelings to think of anything else.

The scent of her skin was driving him mad as he kissed her throat. His hands shook as they caressed her body, and Gina shuddered. This was dangerous. He was getting to her. If she didn't stop him now she had a sinking feeling that she wouldn't be able to stop him at all.

She tensed and then before Nick caught on to what was happening she gave him a violent shove which sent him crashing backwards off the bed.

In the kitchen, Esteban stopped talking and looked round. 'What was that?'

Irena was on her feet, pale and nervous. 'Should we go and see?'

In the bedroom, Nick was on his feet again, scowling at Gina, who had pulled the sheets up to her shoulders. 'What the hell did you do that for?'

'Get out of my bedroom!' was all she said.

'What's the matter with you?' His eyes narrowed, trying to work out her mood. 'Just now you were——'

'Asleep,' she threw back, her face hot and her green eyes furious. 'I was asleep, you bastard, and you took advantage of that! Well, I'm awake now, so buzz off!'

'You may have been sleepy, but you kissed me back!'

'I'd rather kiss a snake!'

'Is that why you've been dating Philip Slade?' he asked nastily and she gave him an icy stare without bothering to reply.

Nick moved restlessly, irritably. He had come so close, for a few moments, had been sure she had finally softened, that he was going to get her at last. Frustration ate at him and he ground his teeth, watching her. She was the most stubborn, maddening...

A pang of pain shot through his back and he winced. Petulantly, he muttered, 'Well, anyway...there was no need to be so violent! I shall be covered in bruises tomorrow.'

'Good!' she callously snapped.

At that instant, Irena pushed the door wide open and stood there, framed in yellow light. 'Is...anything wrong?' she asked uncertainly, looking from one to the other of them. 'We heard a crash.'

'I knocked the lamp over, but it didn't break,' Nick said in an offhand voice. 'I'm afraid I woke Gina up, though.'

'Oh, what a pity,' Irena said, looking at the other girl's flushed face with concern. 'You look so tired, too; almost feverish. I wish I didn't have to tell you, but you'll have to know tomorrow. Gina, they brought bad news—Roz didn't leave the plane, she's still on it.'

Roz was awake, too, curled up in a seat at the front of the plane under the watchful, jumpy eyes of the youngest terrorist. He was on guard while the leader was in the cockpit with the pilot and the third man dozed across three empty seats. The boy's delicate-featured face was ashen with weariness, his eyes like black holes. Most of the passengers were managing to sleep fitfully, because this was their second night on board the plane and they had begun to adjust to their situation more since the women and children left, but Roz was too strung up, and in too much pain, to relax enough even for that.

They had made her move to this seat, where they could watch her, after they discovered that she was a reporter. For half an hour she had been terrified for her life as they barked furious questions at her. Who did she work for? Was she a political journalist? What sort of paper did she write for? What was she doing on this plane? Roz had answered as calmly as she could, but sweat had been running like a river down her back. Any minute, she was expecting to get shot.

They had run out of anger and suspicion in the end, though, and then the leader began a long harangue, which he made her write down—their demands and accusations, their political beliefs, couched in high-flown, inflated language.

Roz had tried to keep her face expressionless, to play them on a long line, but perhaps something in her face betrayed that she was not impressed because the leader had suddenly snarled and pistol-whipped her round the face.

The pain had been so bad that Roz had passed out. When she came to, the three men had moved away, they were talking in a huddle near the cockpit.

Then the leader had gone back to talk to the two pilots, and the older of the other two had allowed a stewardess to do some rough and ready emergency work on her bruised face. The iodine had stung, and the stewardess had asked her sympathetically, 'You OK?'

'I'll live,' Roz had murmured back.

'No whispering!' the young boy had snapped at them then. 'That's enough, go back to your seat, woman!'

Her face still throbbed now, some hours later, but the pain had lessened somewhat. If she looked sideways at the dark window she could see her reflection: her cheek was swollen and bruised, there was a yellow iodine-coloured weal across the redness. I'm not a pretty sight, she thought wryly. Good thing Daniel isn't around to see me.

That was a mistake. She must not think about Daniel. It weakened her, made her eyes blur with tears. Mustn't think about him.

She shut her eyes and thought about her father, instead—was he on his way to Vietnam? Then she thought about poor little Irena, who must be in London and sick with anxiety. You never knew what was going to happen to you from one day to the next, did you? This whole business was like a traffic accident. There she had been, on a routine flight, when suddenly...

That was when all hell broke loose. Dazed and confused, Roz lifted her head and stared as the terrorist leader ran out, screaming orders or swearing, she couldn't tell which. The youngest one swung, staring, trembling violently. The sleeping terrorist fell to the floor and scrambled up again, his gun in his hand, already beginning to shoot.

So many things happened at once that she couldn't untangle the events of those few moments—as the terrorist leader ran into the cabin there had been a smashing sound, the sound of glass breaking in the cockpit, and almost simultaneously the air was full of acrid smoke as smoke bombs were thrown.

Someone, somewhere, shouted, 'Get down, get down! On the floor, get down on the floor!' and at the same time through the smoke loomed soldiers in camouflage uniform, their hands and faces blackened and their eyes strangely white and glittering. The sound of gunfire began as Roz saw them.

She had been so bewildered by the way it had all happened that she hadn't thought of getting down on the floor, and it was only when the terrorist leader turned his gun on her deliberately that she realised the danger she was in. She opened her mouth to scream as the first bullet hit her, and then the shock of the impact silenced her, knocked her silent like a smack in the face, before the second and third bullets sent her sideways and downwards like a sagging doll to lie bleeding and dumb on the floor.

# CHAPTER FIVE

IRENA slept restlessly, moving in and out of strange and terrifying dreams. It seemed an endless night. But she woke up to an English summer morning, the sound of birdsong like high flutes, and through the closed curtains a golden light filtering to flood the walls of her room. She lay in bed, staring around her at these unfamiliar surroundings, slowly remembering everything that had happened since she flew into London—was it only the day before yesterday? It seemed like days, weeks ago. Time had flashed past her as if she was riding a whirlwind.

Roz was still on that plane, she thought with a pang, and in terrible danger. Irena knew she would never be able to cope with what Roz was having to face. She shivered at the very idea and then stiffened, her head lifting to listen, at the same instant realising what had woken her. Someone was ringing the front doorbell of the flat; a loud, prolonged ring. She looked at her wristwatch, which lay on the bedside table. It was still only seven-thirty—who could be ringing at this hour?

Panic surged up inside her. Roz! Something had happened to Roz. What else could it be? She almost fell out of bed and snatched up her dressing-gown, shouldered into it as she stumbled out of the bedroom and up the hall to the front door.

Gina came out of her own room as Irena went past. She, too, was wearing a dressing-gown, and was pale. Their eyes met in shared anxiety, but they didn't speak.

Gina followed her down the hall and pulled open the front door.

Esteban stood outside, pale and drawn, his dark eyes like holes in a blanket.

'What's happened?' Irena burst out. She knew from his expression that he brought bad news.

'Please sit down first,' he said, his voice deep and formal and her terror grew worse.

'She's dead!' she whispered, and heard the intake of his breath.

'No, no!' Esteban put an arm round Irena and forcibly steered her into the sitting-room, made her sit down and then, kneeling in front of her, rubbed her icy hands as if she was a child while he talked in a quiet, soothing voice.

'Keep calm, Irena, don't shake like that. Roz isn't dead, I promise you, but...' He paused, looked up at Gina who had sat down, too, as if she could no longer trust her legs to bear her. He went on roughly, 'Well, the local authorities decided to storm the plane over-night, take the terrorists off guard while they were at their lowest ebb.'

'Oh, no!' Irena cried out, aghast at that news. 'How could they be so reckless? Why couldn't they wait and keep them talking, wear them down until they gave up?'

'I don't know, it's very hard to say what should be done in these circumstances, we don't know all the facts,' said Esteban, shrugging. 'But they took the decision, and in the fighting Roz got shot...'

Irena's grey eyes darkened; she was white. 'Is it bad? I must go to her, I must go there now, at once, be with her.'

Esteban shook his head quickly. 'No, Irena, you can't. It's impossible for you to go out there. Nick is dealing with things—he is at the office now, he left as soon as Daniel's call came through, immediately after the plane was stormed and he heard that Roz had been shot. Nick is making what arrangements he can to fly her home as soon as she can travel—Daniel will be able to give us up-to-date news when he rings again. Nick talked to him on the phone an hour ago—Daniel is at the hospital with her. She hasn't had surgery yet, but I'm afraid an operation is going to be necessary. They are giving her blood at the moment, trying to stabilise her...'

'Oh...' Irena murmured, her eyes closing briefly as that image sank in. It sounded very serious, despite Esteban's attempt to minimise the threat to Roz.

Esteban watched her, frowning. 'Daniel will be in touch if the situation changes in any way at all. Nick asked if you should go over there, and Daniel said no. Things are pretty chaotic at the moment, you would only get in the way.'

She flinched. 'I have a right to be there! She is my sister!'

'Irena, I know how worried you must be,' Esteban said gently, 'but I think you should do as Daniel suggests. He's on the spot, he knows exactly how things stand.'

She looked at him with hostility, her grey eyes flashing like summer lightning. 'Don't give me orders! What is all this to do with you, anyway? Roz is nothing to do with you! Mind your own business! Oh, why don't you go away?'

He stood up, a very tall man, his face graven stone suddenly. 'Nick asked me to break the news to you, rather than let you hear it on TV,' he said coldly. 'Now that I've done that, I'll join Nick at the office. I think you should go back to bed and stay there—I'm sure Mrs

Tyrrell can suggest a doctor who could give you a sedative.'

'I don't want to go back to bed!' she muttered, scowling at him.

He shrugged. 'That is up to you. I've given you my advice, I didn't really expect you to take it.'

He turned on his heel and vanished and Irena burst into tears as the front door banged behind him.

Gina gave her a rueful look. 'It was kind of him to break the news to you, you know. It can't have been an easy job, poor man.'

'I want to go to Roz, Gina. I can't bear being here, while she is so ill and might...' Irena broke off, a sigh wrenching her whole body.

Gina sighed, too. 'I know how you feel, but I expect Daniel is right—you would only be another problem for him to cope with. If Nick means to fly her home, he'll manage it as soon as she is fit to be moved, don't worry.'

'I'm not going back to bed, or doping myself until I don't know what is going on!'

Gina smiled soothingly at her. 'I agree—the worst thing for you would be to sit around brooding. Work will help to keep your mind off your worries. Come into the office; at least we'll hear any news long before we would get it from the TV. Why don't you have a shower and get dressed while I make some coffee and breakfast?'

'I'm not hungry!'

Gina eyed her with wry uncertainty. 'Why are you so obstinate? But I should be used to the stubborn way your family acts. You and Roz have that in common, you're both pig-headed.'

Irena laughed a little at that, which made it easier to persuade her to do what Gina asked. She had a shower, then put on a lavender and white summer dress. While

she was brushing her long, smooth brown hair the news
started on TV, and the hijacking story was the lead. The
screen was full of images which chilled her blood: the
plane on the tarmac, smoke billowing from it, armed
soldiers swarming up the steps, ambulances and fire engines wailing up to surround the plane and a later film
of the sheeted bodies of the terrorists being removed.
They had all, it seemed, been killed. Irena shivered.

'Injured passengers have all been taken to the nearest
hospital for emergency treatment,' the newsreader calmly
said. 'Any relatives may ring the following telephone
numbers for information...'

Irena scrabbled in her purse for a pen, to write down
the numbers, although she knew that she would get far
more detailed information from the foreign desk on the
*Sentinel*. When the news ended, she switched off the TV
and went to the kitchen to join Gina, who looked at her
searchingly. Irena's dress was delicate and pretty, but it
emphasised the fact that she had no colour this morning,
and there were dark circles under her big grey eyes. She
ought to eat, but Gina decided not to force the issue.
What Irena needed was to be soothed, reassured, not
argued with. So she poured Irena some coffee and added
cream and sugar, and at least Irena drank that with an
absent-minded expression.

It wasn't until they were on their way to the office that
a sudden thought occurred to Gina. 'I can't understand
how Nick and Esteban get up to the apartment, you
know. Has Nick been bribing the security man, I
wonder? Nobody is supposed to be allowed up to my
floor without my express permission. I must look into
that.'

Irena gave her a startled look. 'Nick didn't tell you?
He says he has bought the other flat on your floor.'

Gina stiffened, turning pale. 'What?' Her mind raced with all the implications of the news. Nick had invaded her private territory!

She had felt safe up there, behind security locks, with no other tenant on her floor except the man who never seemed to come to London. She could close her door and be sure of being alone, free from any intrusion. But not any more. Nick was going to be there every day, right next door, too close for comfort. She felt a pang of helplessness. Nick didn't let up, did he? She kept forgetting that nature of his—forgetting that he was a man driven to win. He never admitted defeat or gave up until he got what he wanted.

A shiver ran through her, her face flushed then whitened, remembering the half-dreaming, half-waking sweetness of those moments on her bed. She knew what she wanted, too, but there were some things you could pay too high a price for.

She had had an ineradicable glimpse of Nick's bedrock nature when he broke his word to the old man she loved and tried to gain control of the *Sentinel* behind their backs. Nick was ruthlessly set on getting his own way, making everyone do what he wanted, including her— and Gina was equally set on denying him that satisfaction, in every sense of the word.

There had been a time when she had suspected Nick of only pretending to find her attractive, but she knew now that that wasn't true. She didn't believe he loved her; she had come to doubt that he was capable of loving anyone except himself. He wanted her, though; she had felt his frustration last night, burning like a furnace, and it made her body tremble to remember, because she couldn't quite get over Nick.

He was under her skin, a bitter thorn, and his passion was a temptation—even if it wasn't the sort of love she had once been fool enough to dream he might give her.

She had hoped she would forget him, by dating Philip Slade, but that had been a waste of time. Philip was pleasant enough, but he was immature, a selfish and spoilt young man who had never grown up. She still dated him only because he made a useful smoke-screen and he kept asking her out. She knew Philip didn't love her, so he wouldn't get hurt, but she had sworn to make Nick pay for Sir George's death, and she hoped that watching her with another man might at least annoy Nick. It certainly seemed to!

When she and Irena arrived at Barbary Wharf they walked into a major security check. 'I'm sorry, Mrs Tyrrell,' the head of security said as he glanced at her identity card. 'We had a bomb scare earlier and we're on red alert. Probably a hoax, but with what's going on in Cyprus, and our Miss Amery getting shot like that, we can't be too careful.'

'Quite right, Mr Brown,' Gina smiled at him. 'You wouldn't be doing your job if you didn't take precautions.'

He looked at Irena, eyes narrowing. 'I don't think we've seen you before, miss, have we?'

'This is Roz Amery's half-sister, Irena,' Gina told him.

He stared at Irena with sympathy and faint curiosity. 'Pleased to meet you, miss, I'm sure. I was very shocked to hear Miss Amery had been shot, we're all keeping our fingers crossed for her. I hope we'll have good news soon.'

'Thank you,' Irena said huskily.

She had rung the emergency number given out on television, before she and Gina left the apartment, but they had had no news to give her other than that Roz was comfortable, and would probably be undergoing surgery. Irena had asked a lot of questions, and got no answers. They wouldn't even tell her how many times, or in what part of her body, Roz had been shot.

The security man coughed. 'Sorry to ask, but...I'm afraid I have to see your identity card, miss. Just a formality. We have to stick to the rules, even if we know someone personally, miss.'

'I haven't been issued with one, yet,' Irena said, looking at Gina helplessly. 'I have my passport and my French identity card...'

'French identity card?' he repeated, looking puzzled.

'She works in Paris usually,' Gina said. 'Don't worry, I'll vouch for her, Mr Brown.'

'Well, I don't know...' He frowned.

Gina looked bland. 'Or you can get Mr Caspian himself down to do it! He knows her.'

'Oh, that won't be necessary,' Mr Brown said at once, as she had known he would.

Everyone who worked at Barbary Wharf, from the highest to the lowest, was scared stiff of Nick Caspian and reluctant to clash with him. They had learnt very quickly to fear him; he had been through their ranks like frost in May, scything down numberless members of staff, and anyone who wanted to keep their job was ready to do almost anything to please him now. Gina grimly reflected that she was probably the only person on the staff who was prepared to cross him, whatever the consequences, but then she did not need to fear him. Nick couldn't sack her.

'But please make sure she gets her security card today, won't you?' Mr Brown added in a formal voice.

'I will,' promised Gina, smiling soothingly at him.

Irena followed Gina into the busy, marble-floored foyer, across which streams of people flowed to and from the lifts. Her large grey eyes were bemused. She saw plate-glass doors standing open at one end of the echoing foyer, and through them glimpsed flowers, sunshine, an open, paved square.

'The plaza,' Gina reminded. 'The night you arrived you had dinner here, remember?'

Irena nodded. 'The open square, where Daniel and I ate!'

'See the green blinds of Pierre's place? That's where you and Daniel had dinner.'

Irena had only the most confused memory of that night because so much had happened to her since. By now, she couldn't even remember what she had eaten for dinner. One memory was sharp enough, though—bleak, dark eyes which had looked at her with biting contempt.

Esteban! It was a name she had always liked, the Spanish for Stephen. A romantic name, she had thought it. It suited him. He was a very attractive man, in spite of his brooding air and a smouldering anger she sensed hidden inside him.

At first it had puzzled her, until he broke out with his accusations—but she still didn't understand what on earth had given him the impression that she and Daniel were involved, or why the thought should make him so furious.

Anyone who knew Daniel and Roz would realise that they were totally wrapped up in each other. Yet he seemed to know them well enough, which made his anger odd, unless...

Irena broke off, her brown furrowed. Surely Esteban wasn't secretly interested in Roz? Well, that might make

some sense—if he was angry because he thought Daniel
was cheating on her? But if he was interested in Roz,
surely he would have been pleased if he suspected Daniel
was looking elsewhere?

For some reason she found the idea that Esteban might
be attracted to Roz disturbing—but what other expla-
nation could there be for his rage that night?

He was a Spanish man, of course, and took himself
very seriously. Even today, Spanish men were brought
up to be very aware of their male dignity; they still clung
to the old ideas about the way a man behaved, about
honour and tradition, and respect for the family, and
Irena had a certain inbred sympathy for their attitudes.
She had grown up with them, after all.

She remembered how her father had always reacted,
living up to his own image of what a man should be!
Her brothers were of another generation, but in many
ways they were the same. A lot had changed in Spain,
but you couldn't alter overnight the way men thought,
and Esteban might have jumped to the wrong con-
clusion about her and Daniel because buried inside his
head was an archetypal image of what the male-female
relationship meant. Seeing Daniel with another woman,
in an intimate mood, could easily have suggested that
he was being unfaithful to Roz.

Well, at least he had been set right about his stupid
suspicions, and he had had the grace to apologise! Irena
thought, flushed and still angry.

Gina had gone on talking, unaware that Irena wasn't
listening. 'And over there is the snack bar, Torelli's—
you can buy take-out food there; sandwiches and salads
and fruit. Old Mrs Torelli is usually there, or her son
Roberto. They're both very friendly. Sometimes, we buy
a snack and sit in the Ratcliff Walk gardens to eat it.

And you can get a taxi in North Street, and there's a bus-stop in Silver Street, that's the first left, going out of the side-gate.'

Gina looked round then, and gave Irena a wry grin, seeing her dazed expression.

'Well, never mind, you'll soon find your way around.'

She walked towards the steel-doored lifts, with Irena following, and a moment later they were on the directorial floor.

'This is my office,' Gina said, pushing open a door. There was a girl standing beside one of the large windows, watering house plants. She half turned, smiling, the sun haloing her brown hair in shining gold.

Irena liked her at first sight. She had a direct way of looking at you, her eyes light grey, her smile warm and friendly.

'Hazel, this is Roz's half-sister, Irena,' Gina said, and Hazel Forbes gave Irena a startled, sympathetic look.

'Of course, I heard you were coming to work here for the summer. Poor you, you haven't had a very happy start, have you? I'm so sorry about Roz, but Daniel rang a moment ago and said that she was out of the operating theatre and the doctors are quite hopeful, so that's better news, isn't it?'

Irena's grey eyes opened wide, her pale face began to glow with returning colour. 'That's wonderful! Oh, I wish I had been here, I could have talked to Daniel. Did he leave a number? Can we ring him back?'

'Oh, dear, I am sorry. Daniel said we weren't to try to ring him—it's impossible at the moment, things are pretty chaotic in the hospital, I gather, and he's going to stay there, to be around when Roz regains consciousness. He said he would ring again in a couple of hours, though—and he left you a message: you're not to worry, she's holding her own and he'll keep in touch.'

Irena sighed. 'Oh, well, I'll just have to be patient, won't I?'

Hazel smiled at her reassuringly. 'Afraid so.'

Irena picked up a magazine lying on Hazel's desk and stared at the cover, which showed a bride in full regalia—floor-length, full-skirted white silk gown, long veil, a tiara of pearls and orange blossoms, a large bouquet of white flowers.

'Oh, a bridal magazine! Is someone getting married?' she asked casually, and Hazel blushed.

'I am, in a couple of weeks—I hope you'll come. It is going to be a Caspian International wedding! My fiancé, Piet, has worked for Nick Caspian for years, so Nick has accepted an invitation, and Gina is going to be matron of honour. We're hoping Roz will be well enough to be one of my bridesmaids, even if she comes in a wheelchair! You'll be able to meet all Roz's friends.'

'Thank you, I'd love to go,' Irena said, surprised and touched by the invitation from someone she had only just met. Everyone in London seemed so friendly—look at the way Gina had taken care of her when they hardly knew each other!

Later, Gina took her down to the personnel officer to fill in a form, after which Irena was despatched to have her photograph taken, since her security card needed an up-to-date photo of her. The picture desk editor, Tim Doyle, was in his office, his desk spread with glossy black and white pictures, moving them around in what seemed a haphazard fashion. A long, thin, lugubrious man of around fifty, in a black shirt and grey trousers, and a well-washed pea-green wool cardigan which reached his knees, he was oblivious of Irena until she tapped shyly on his open door. Then he looked up. 'Hi, come in! What can I do for you?'

'I've been sent here to have my photo taken,' Irena huskily told him.

'Why and who sent you?'

'Personnel, I need a picture for my security card.'

Tim Doyle laughed shortly, with irritation. 'You're kidding! You're not? Go back to Personnel and tell them this department isn't here to take cheap passport pictures. Go out to Woolworths in your lunch break, and use their photo booth—everyone else does.'

Irena was confused, but obediently turned to leave, not liking to argue with him in case her English was not up to the job. Tim Doyle watched her go, and then suddenly called after her, 'Hang on a minute!' and she turned to look enquiringly at him.

He stared fixedly at her, from head to foot, then looked down to the photos on his desk. 'Who are you, did you say?' he murmured absently, and before she could answer, 'Just started, have you? What's your name and where are you going to be working?'

'I am Irena Olivero,' she said in husky, formal English. 'I started work today, I am only working here for the summer, translating.'

Tim Doyle looked at her thoughtfully. 'Student?'

She nodded, her long brown hair swishing against her cheeks.

'Where do you come from, darling? Italy?'

'I am Spanish, but I am studying in Paris,' she politely explained, looking at her watch. 'Excuse me, please, I think I should go back and explain to Personnel that I have to go out to have my photo taken.'

Tim Doyle smiled coaxingly, all charm suddenly. 'That's all right, darling, I'll make an exception for you—hold on while I get someone to come and take a few snaps of you.' He looked out of his office and shouted, 'Hey, Simon! Come here, will you? I've got a little job for you.'

A young man with smooth good looks, pale blond hair, blue eyes, wearing what Irena immediately recognised as very fashionable clothes, appeared in the doorway, gave Irena an interested look, then said to Tim Doyle, 'What do you want?'

'Take some snaps of this young lady for us, will you, Simon? The little studio's free, use that.' He smiled at Irena. 'Happy now, darling? Right, off you go, then.'

She thanked him politely and left his office with the younger man following her, but suddenly Tim Doyle called after them.

'Just a minute, Simon, can I have a private word? Wait out there, would you, miss? Won't be a second.'

The blond young man went back into the office and Irena waited, looking around the room with some curiosity. She was looking forward to beginning work here on the *Sentinel*, but already she had seen so many different departments, met so many people, that she was feeling rather battered and confused, and the one place she had not seen was the foreign desk translation unit where she would be working.

She looked back at the picture desk editor's office and saw the two men staring at her. Why had that man changed his mind, she wondered? What was he talking to the other man about, and why on earth were they staring at her like that?

'Come on,' Simon said, emerging from the office and sliding a familiar hand through her arm. 'Let's get to work, shall we? What's your name?'

'Irena,' she said and he gave her a thoughtful look.

'Old-fashioned, haven't heard it for years—but I like it. It suits you, you've got an old-fashioned look, especially in that dress—dim and shadowy, like a flower garden hidden by high walls. I like that, could be quite sexy, if we shoot it in the right way...'

Irena was totally baffled. What was he talking about? Didn't he understand that she only wanted three head-and-shoulder shots of herself for her security pass? Hadn't the picture desk editor explained?

'I have to get back to the office quite soon,' she said. 'They only want head and shoulder shots. It's vital that I am in the office in an hour.' Daniel was going to ring again then, and she had to talk to him, she must know how seriously Roz had been wounded.

'Oh, sure,' Simon said. 'Of course, whatever you say, darling.'

Irena could tell he wasn't even listening.

Back in Gina's office, Hazel was on the phone to Piet in Utrecht when Esteban knocked on the door and walked into the room a second later without waiting.

Hazel looked up and waved a friendly hand. 'Do you want me?' she mouthed, and Esteban glanced around the room, and, seeing nobody else, nodded. He had been expecting to find Gina here, but presumably she was with Nick in the chairman's office.

Hazel stifled a sigh, and said into the phone, 'Sorry, darling, I must go, the marketing director has just arrived. Yes, Esteban. Yes, I'll say hello to him for you. Tell him what? Oh, OK. Talk to you later, darling. Bye.'

She put the phone down and swung round in her chair to face Esteban, her hands flat on her desk. 'You heard? Piet says hello, and he hopes you're enjoying working in London.'

'That is very friendly of him.' Esteban gave one of his grave smiles. He had met Piet only a few times, but he liked him. Most people did. Piet had an easygoing nature which made him very likeable, especially as he was non-competitive in a company full of very ambitious people.

'He's a very friendly guy,' said Hazel with pride. 'Oh, and he said to tell you he loved your latest book, *The Sentinel Book of World Architecture*. The glossy pictures were gorgeous, and he approved of the articles; you got some very sound people to write for you.'

Esteban gave her a wry look. 'Good of him to say so, but actually I had nothing to do with the conception of it, my predecessor had the original idea and pushed it through. By the time I arrived the book was finished and in proof.'

Hazel gave him a shrewd, thoughtful look. She was used to people being ready to claim the credit for work they hadn't done; it was rare to meet someone so determined to set the record straight. Hazel approved of Esteban, and could see why Piet liked him. 'How's the book selling?'

'Preliminary sales look good, and judging by the sales of other Sentinel World Books we should do very well. The historical atlas sold like hot cakes, as you know, and the European trade atlas is doing even better. I'm reliably informed it is required reading in most of the stock markets of the world.'

'It looked pretty dull to me!' Hazel admitted, and Esteban gave a sudden, charming smile.

'It isn't what you might call a coffee-table book!'

Hazel laughed. 'No, it is not! I hear you're making big changes in marketing!'

'I've had to shed some staff, to meet Mr Caspian's guidelines, and we're working on some new projects, like the *Sentinel* calendar.' Esteban's voice was flat and cool and Hazel picked up a distinct impression that he did not approve of the calendar.

'Oh, the *Sentinel* girls?' She pulled a face. 'I don't know that I like the idea, myself. It will make Sir George turn in his grave.' She swung in her chair and knocked her bridal magazine off her desk. Esteban bent to pick it up and looked at it, smiling.

'When does Piet return to London for the wedding?'

Hazel sighed. 'Not for two weeks. He is still busy with this Utrecht project—the printing works Caspian International is building. Piet is in charge, and can't get away yet.'

'You are going to be missed in this office!' Esteban said politely.

'Oh, I'm not going anywhere!'

'But . . . after you are married? What will you and Piet do?'

'I shall stay on here for a while, at least. I shall just go over to Utrecht to be with Piet every weekend, I suppose.'

Esteban stared at her, his dark eyes sombre. 'That sort of arrangement does not work well, Hazel, take my word for it. Marriage is no easy matter at the best of times, but if you want it to work you have to be together all the time, or you run the risk of your marriage breaking up . . .'

He broke off, frowning, and she stared at him curiously. She barely knew the man but she sensed that he was talking personally. Was he married, had his marriage broken up because he had left his wife behind in Spain? There had been whispers that he was married, but he hadn't brought a wife with him and nobody knew much about him. He wasn't easy to get to know—rather remote, although he was certainly handsome, if you liked the Mediterranean type: sleek black hair and tanned skin, and those dark eyes. Hazel preferred blonds, like Piet; she had liked him on sight. She wasn't attracted by Esteban, although she knew plenty of girls who were.

Valerie Knight, for one, she thought, secretly amused. She had flipped over Esteban the first time she saw him, and she still seemed very interested. Maybe Valerie knew more about his private life?

Esteban looked at the clock and Hazel followed his glance, frowning. 'Time's getting on. I wonder what's happened to Irena? She's having her photo taken for a security pass, but she should be here now, Daniel is going to ring through with the latest news of Roz at midday.'

'It's ten to twelve? I'll see if I can find her, she mustn't miss Daniel's call.'

'No need for you to go, I'll ring the picture desk, and remind her,' Hazel said, but spoke to the empty air. Esteban had already gone.

When he walked out of the lift on the editorial floor he ran into Valerie Knight, who smiled delightedly. 'Hello, Esteban! I haven't seen you for days—have you been busy?'

'Very,' he said, poised to hurry past to the picture desk office.

'With the *Sentinel* calendar?' Her violet eyes gleamed with laughter.

Esteban nodded curtly and she gave him a wicked look.

'You know, someone threatened to send in a snap of me in a bikini, but I told him it was against the rules, as I work for the paper.'

'I'm afraid so,' Esteban said, and she lowered her lashes, watching him through them.

'I don't suppose they would have used it, anyway!'

He laughed suddenly. 'Now, Valerie, you know the Picture Desk would love to print a picture of you in a bikini! If anything would sell papers, that would!'

'I'm flattered!' she said, laughing softly, delighted with having got the compliment she had been angling for. He was so gorgeous, the perfect foil to her own colouring, and he was a difficult fish to catch, elusive and hard to understand. Valerie was used to landing men without even trying; the fact that she was having trouble getting Esteban made her all the more determined to get him in the end.

Esteban watched her, thinking that it was a pity they couldn't use her—she was sexier than any of the girls whose photos had been picked so far. He had always found blonde hair sexy, and Valerie's figure would make any man's head spin.

But time was running out; he looked at his watch and grimaced. 'Sorry, have to rush . . .'

Valerie's mouth turned down as he hurried away. He was off the hook again! And just when she thought he might ask her out to dinner! He was an infuriating man!

A meeting of editorial heads of department was just finishing in the boardroom; everyone was filing out, talking to each other as they went, still absorbed in the discussion that had occupied them for the last hour, Nick's desire to change the image the *Sentinel* had had for years, update it and broaden its appeal to the buying public.

Only Nick and Gina were left sitting at the long, highly polished table, gathering up their piles of documents. They had clashed again, during the meeting, over Nick's plans. Gina hated the idea of any change for the *Sentinel*; she was flushed and very irritated.

'Thought any more about this west coast trip?' Nick asked curtly as Gina got up to go, her sheaf of papers under her arm.

'I've had other things on my mind,' she snapped. 'While Roz was in danger I couldn't think about anything else.'

Nick inclined his head. 'Yes, it has been a worrying time, but it's over now. Roz is tough, she takes after her father; she'll be OK.'

Gina gave him an impatient look. 'I wish I was as certain as you are. I'm on tenterhooks to hear Daniel's latest news—he's ringing at noon. I must get back to the office.'

Nick followed her towards the door, his long legs easily keeping pace with her. 'Gina,' he muttered, 'I want you to come on this trip. It will help you to get a clear idea of how Caspian International works, of our thinking as a company.'

'I've already got a pretty fair idea of your thinking,' Gina angrily told him. 'You gave us a demonstration just now, in that meeting. You know what Sir George would say if he had been there? He would say you were turning what had been a good, honest newspaper into a cheap and trashy tabloid! You don't care how vulgar it is, so long as it sells in millions, do you?'

'There's nothing vulgar about selling in millions, Gina,' he retorted impatiently. 'We are there to give the public what they want.'

'Crude photos of half-naked girls?'

'They're not crude, they're artistic,' Nick said with a mocking grin.

Gina snorted. 'They're soft porn!'

'Don't be such a puritan! Go to any beach in July and you would see as much!'

'That's different,' she said angrily.

'Why?'

'Because . . . because it is!' she said. 'Sir George would hate it if he knew what you were doing!'

'Sir George was out of touch with the modern newspaper business, but he had an excuse. He was an old man. You're still young, you can still learn.'

'I don't want to learn to think like you!' she snapped at him and a dark flush rose in his face, she saw his eyes glitter and was glad that she had pierced that tough ego of his.

'Well, if you want to understand the modern newspaper business you're going to have to discover more about Caspian International,' he said sharply. 'And I want you in California on this trip. It is time you discovered what Caspian International is about. Either come, or admit that you aren't interested in the company, and give up your seat on the board.'

She stiffened, meeting the angry challenge of his eyes. After a second she shrugged. 'Very well, if you insist, I'll come.'

She caught the triumphant gleam before he looked away, his body relaxing a little. 'Good,' he said offhandedly. 'Oh, and while we're in California you must meet my mother.'

She gave him a startled look, her voice unconsciously cool. 'Meet your mother?'

Her tone offended him, his temper flashed up to boiling point again. 'If you don't want to meet her, forget I suggested it!'

Before Gina could get another word out he was gone, striding out of sight so fast that he had vanished a second later. She felt like bursting into tears. Lately, Nick was as unpredictable as a volcano—dormant and apparently safe one minute, and then suddenly exploding for no reason. You had to watch every word you said to him.

A frown creased her forehead. Was something seriously wrong? With Nick? Or Caspian International? It wasn't like him to be so volatile; there had to be a reason why he was so touchy.

In the hospital in Cyprus, Daniel was sitting beside Roz's bed, holding her hand, although she was unconscious and totally unaware that he was there. Her face was almost as white as the pillow underneath her head, although she had had two blood transfusions since she was brought to the hospital. Daniel had given blood for her once, very glad that they turned out to be the same blood-group.

He had wanted to donate blood for her the second time, but the doctors had turned him down because it would have meant giving blood twice in twenty-four hours and they believed that to be dangerous. Daniel had protested that he was fine, it wouldn't be a problem because he was very fit and in good shape, but they had been adamant. They had tapped other sources of blood for her.

He watched her fixedly, his eyes heavy, red and sore with lack of sleep. He had not slept since he arrived, although he wasn't really conscious of his weariness. He was too intent on Roz. When she was awake she was so full of life, always rushing everywhere, fierce and spitting with energy—but in that bed he became aware that she was tiny and fragile, his Roz, with fine little bones, small hands and feet, she hardly weighed as much as a child, but to Daniel she was the loveliest thing he had ever seen. *Rosa mundi*, rose of the world, he thought.

It was hard to believe that anything so delicate could have stood up to the ordeal of those hours in the plane, but Daniel had heard from some of the unhurt survivors stories of Roz standing up to the terrorists, Roz talking to them in French, writing down what they wanted her to write, sounding and looking very calm and unafraid even in the face of angry, violent threats.

Daniel had always been terrified of something like this happening to her. She had been so hooked on imitating her father, becoming another Des Amery, going boldly where nobody else dared go, risking life and limb in the dangerous places of the earth. Roz loved that damned father of hers, that was the trouble, Daniel thought grimly, and Des was quite a guy, who could deny it? Not Daniel, who had always respected, even revered the man. But when Des Amery threatened Roz's safety Daniel was ready to hate him, and he was certainly prepared to fight him, or rather the image he had left on Roz, the very memory of him, for possession of his daughter's love. Des himself, as Daniel knew, had never wanted Roz to follow in his footsteps, although he had not discouraged her. Des didn't believe in interfering in what his daughter did; he always said that he would have been perfectly happy if she had chosen to take up any other job. No, it was what Des meant to Roz that Daniel had to fight.

A nurse appeared beside him, thin and slight with black hair and eyes. 'You asked me to let you know when it was time for you to make your call to London,' she said gently, and Daniel nodded, getting up.

He laid down Roz's limp hand. Her lids stayed down. She was unmoving.

The nurse watched him with sympathy. 'She isn't going to recover consciousness for a few more hours,' she assured him.

'I know,' said Daniel, but was still reluctant to leave Roz, even for a short time. It was like walking out on his own life. He had never realised how much he cared about her until he thought he might be going to lose her.

The nurse smiled at him, approving of his unwearying devotion to his woman. 'She will be OK, you know,' she said. 'It will take time, but she will be OK.'

Daniel gave her a lopsided, charming grin, touched by her sympathy. 'How soon before she could get married?'

'Next week!' the nurse said, laughing, and thought that if she had been the woman in that bed she would have forced herself to get up to marry him even if she had been dying.


It had taken Esteban some time to track Irena down, but eventually he discovered the small studio adjacent to the picture desk developing room, and walked into the room just in time to see the photographer busily arranging a confused-looking Irena on a dais so that she would lean on an artificial almond tree in profuse pink silk bloom.

'Can we just push your skirt aside a little? We need to see your beautiful legs, this skirt is far too long. And I think we need a couple of these buttons undone...now, darling, don't be silly,' Simon said as Irena slapped his hands away. 'Anyone would think I was trying to rape you!' He laughed cheerfully, but Irena wasn't amused.

She had forgotten her English, she was stammering angrily in Spanish, very pink and distressed after half an hour of what she increasingly realised was not the sort of photographic session she had expected.

Esteban broke into this scene, his face hard and angry as he strode over to the dais. 'What's going on here?' he demanded in English.

'Who the hell are you?' Simon snapped back, swinging round to glare at this stranger who had interrupted his work. 'How did you get in here? Can't you read? There's a sign on the door that says private, no entry.'

'I am the marketing director. I don't need permission to walk in here,' Esteban bit out, his black eyes dangerous as they met those of the other man.

Simon let go of Irena and forced a placating smile. 'Oh, sir... Sorry, I didn't recognise you.' He certainly didn't want to offend a man as important as the marketing director, who, after all, was in control of this entire project, and could make or break Simon's career.

Esteban caught hold of Irena's arm and pulled her free, shaking her slightly, as if he was furious with her and would have liked to slap her.

'Daniel will be coming through any second now; you have to get up to Mrs Tyrrell's office.' He propelled her towards the door, and Simon followed them, protesting.

'But sir, we haven't finished this session——'

'Oh, yes, you have,' Esteban said, giving him a look that silenced him, and then Irena found herself being pushed through the studio door and along a corridor towards a lift.

She tried to break free of Esteban's hard, punitive fingers, but he refused to let go of her. He pressed the lift button, his face averted, and she looked sideways at him nervously.

'Thank you for——' She broke off in alarm as she caught the angry flash of his dark eyes.

'How could you let him paw you?'

'I...I didn't...' she protested.

'Don't lie to me! I saw what was going on as I walked in... he had his hands all over you!'

He looked down at the bodice of her dress, his brows black and heavy over his contemptuous eyes. 'And do up those buttons, before someone else sees you!'

Irena's skin was burning hot and her hands trembled as she tried to do up her buttons, her head hanging. She felt like crying, but not with Esteban watching her in that angry, disgusted fashion.

The lift arrived and Esteban caught hold of her elbow, propelled her into the lift as if she was likely to try to escape. She was still fumbling with her buttons as the lift door shut, and he abruptly pushed her hands out of the way and she felt his cool fingers brushing her skin as he deftly finished buttoning her dress.

She couldn't look at him, her eyes down, her lashes brushing her hot cheeks.

'I suppose you're the age to want to experience everything,' he said harshly. 'But you can get yourself into trouble that way, especially with opportunistic men like that one...'

'I only wanted——' Irena began in a low, husky voice, trying to explain that she had gone there to have a quick snapshot of her head and shoulders for her security pass, but Esteban didn't let her finish.

'I know what you wanted!' He pushed her against the wall of the lift, his hands gripping her shoulders, and Irena drew a shaken breath as his mouth swooped down, crushing her parted lips. She had never been kissed like that before; the force and hunger in the kiss clouded her mind, made her tremble violently.

Then the lift stopped, the doors opened, and Esteban let go of her, turning on his heel to walk away without giving her a second look. Shaky and dazed, Irena stumbled down the corridor to Gina's office. Esteban had already vanished elsewhere.

Gina and Hazel looked up, startled, as she opened the door, then smiled. 'Did you get your photos done?'

'Not really,' she huskily said, but before they could ask any more questions the phone rang.

'Daniel!' Gina said, snatching up the phone, her face alight, and in her eagerness to hear about Roz Irena forgot everything else.

# CHAPTER SIX

WHEN Roz opened her eyes the first thing she saw was Daniel—fast asleep beside her bed, his dark head resting on the back of a very uncomfortable-looking chair.

Roz closed her eyes again almost immediately, believing she was hallucinating, as she had so often on the plane, when thinking of Daniel had been something she tried to avoid because it made her cry.

But something had been different; was she still on the plane? She retained an impression of whiteness, of more light than she had been expecting.

The last thing she remembered was . . . She frowned and the movement of her brows hurt. She had a headache; her head was banging like a drum. She didn't want to think, she was frightened of what she might remember. Her head rang with worrying sounds: gunfire, screaming, shouting, glass smashing. It was coming back in a flood and she trembled, remembering.

There had been shots. Her body jerked in terrified mimicry. Yes, that was what had happened. She had been shot; over and over again she felt the bullets hitting her, her body jolting backward in recoil. Fear welled up, she was in panic, her heart going much too fast, deafening her.

She had to stop thinking, this was worrying, it was too scary. She had to get herself under control.

She froze in the bed, eyes shut, listening. Where was she? What was happening around her?

Slowly her mind picked up the sounds of the busy hospital. The rattle of trolleys, the slap of the ward doors swinging shut, the squeak of nurses' rubber-soled shoes, the sound of someone coughing, the distant ring of a telephone.

Such ordinary sounds; safe and mundane and wonderful. They made her heart turn over. She opened her eyes and she was not on the plane on the tarmac, she was not lying there bleeding—she was in a hospital bed and Daniel was there, really there.

She gazed at him, trembling. Daniel was right beside her, so close that she could touch him—but he was unaware of her at that instant. Daniel was asleep, with his mouth open, breathing heavily.

'Oh, darling,' Roz whispered, afraid of waking him up, just looking at him with intense happiness. This was not how she had imagined he would look when she saw him again. But it was wonderful. Her heart squeezed inside her chest. He looked touchingly unaware, his body heavy, completely relaxed in sleep, like a little boy, and her love was deeper at that moment than it had ever been before.

Her blue eyes drifted down over him passionately, his face, his broad shoulders, his chest and those slim hips—she had been longing to see him for what seemed years and here he was, not even knowing she was there, and she could look at him as much as she liked.

Then she suddenly realised that he was holding her hand, and she had the feeling that he had been holding it for hours. His hand fitted so beautifully into hers, his skin warm and intimate on her own, as if they had been like that all their lives.

She looked at the two hands lying linked on the spotless white bedspread. 'Oh, my darling,' she whispered again, her thumb lightly stroking the back of his hand, feeling the dark hairs which grew down from his wrist shiver against her skin.

Perhaps it was that touch which made Daniel shift in his sleep and then wake up. His eyelids flickered and then opened, he yawned, and then sat up in the chair, closing his mouth.

That was when he saw Roz. For a moment they stared into each other's eyes in utter silence, and then she gave a quivering little smile and Daniel groaned.

'Roz!'

'Hi,' she said, almost dumb with all those feelings welling up inside her.

Daniel was just as tongue-tied. 'You finally woke up!' he said, his hand almost crushing her small fingers.

Roz nodded. 'Have I been asleep long?'

'Sleeping Beauty had nothing on you!'

She grinned. 'Didn't Prince Charming wake her with a kiss?'

'Did I forget to do that?' he asked huskily and leaned over.

Their mouths met and clung and then Roz gave a faint cry of pain.

'Darling, did I hurt your shoulder?' Daniel asked, his face pale and anxious.

'It doesn't matter,' she said, still wincing.

'I'm sorry, how could I be so clumsy?' Daniel was angry with himself but she smiled at him.

'You forgot—so did I.' She looked down her nose to see what injuries she had and saw the bandages on her arm, across her chest and shoulder. 'This is dramatic!' she said lightly. 'Have I had an operation?'

'Last night,' Daniel nodded. 'They had to take out three bullets and put in some stitches to sew you up again.'

'But the bullets didn't hit anything vital? I don't feel at all bad, except for a headache.'

'You had two bullets in your shoulder, one in your arm, and you lost a lot of blood, but a couple of blood transfusions put that right.'

Roz was still squinting down at herself. 'What about this bandage on my chest?'

'A scratch,' Daniel said. 'A bullet seems to have skated along the side of your chest without entering anywhere.'

'Well, that was lucky,' Roz said with a grin. 'So, Doctor, how am I doing?'

'How do you feel?' Daniel asked, his dark eyes dangerous-looking suddenly.

Roz considered his face and gave him a rueful look. 'Honestly? I feel lucky, darling. Lucky to be alive. I thought I might be going to die and it was not a great feeling, let me tell you!'

'Good,' Daniel said explosively, the anger flashing out of him then. 'It was pretty hellish for me, too, Roz, wondering if you were going to die. I never want to go through the last couple of days again. When you can get out of that bed I am taking you home and from now on you don't go anywhere without me even if I have to chain you to my wrist.'

Roz lay back against her pillows, her dark blue eyes brilliant in her pale face. 'You know, when I was on that plane I knew I might never see you again, and it was the worst thing about it all—until then I didn't realise just how much I love you, Daniel,' she said softly.

He looked down into her passionate dark blue eyes, and gave a rough sigh, then he lifted her hand to his lips and kissed it.

'Roz, will you marry me?'

'Yes, please,' she said.

A few days later, Daniel rang Irena, after he had been sent out of Roz's room while she was being examined by her surgeon and a team of his students.

Irena was in Gina's office, alone, waiting for Gina to come out of a meeting which had taken up her entire afternoon. Hazel had gone home a few moments earlier because she had so many things to do in preparation for her wedding in eight days' time.

When Daniel told her Roz was recovering well now and likely to be allowed to fly home soon, tears sprang into Irena's eyes. 'Oh, that's wonderful. Are you sure, Daniel?'

Daniel's voice was strong and sure, filled with warmth. 'She is going to be fine now, Irena, you can stop worrying about her. I think, with any luck, she'll be able to fly home in time for Hazel's wedding, although she may have to make the trip in a wheelchair. By the day itself, though, she should be just fine.'

He was laughing and Irena laughed too, even while she was running her hand across her wet eyes.

'I'll tell Hazel. She'll be delighted to hear that.'

'Isn't she there?'

'No, she has gone home, and Gina is still in a late meeting, with Mr Caspian and the advertising department and marketing people.'

Irena was picking up the jargon, her English improving by leaps and bounds with practice, although she still had to concentrate hard before she spoke.

'Of course!' groaned Daniel. 'I've lost all sense of time—I forgot that the offices would be closing up and only the editorial departments would be operating.'

'Do you want me to transfer you to the foreign desk?'

'Not tonight,' Daniel said. 'I've filed my copy for today. I'd better get back to Roz now, Irena. I want to know what the surgeon thinks about her condition.'

'Give her my love.'

'I will, of course, and she sends you her love. She said to tell you that she's very sorry to have spoilt your London visit by getting hijacked and shot.'

Irena giggled. 'Tell her I know she was just showing off.'

Daniel laughed. 'Typical Amery fireworks. Yes, Irena, exactly. Well, goodnight, give Roz's love to Gina, too, and she's looking forward to a chat on the phone, maybe tomorrow, if she's up to it.'

Irena replaced the phone, smiling to herself. Daniel sounded happier than he had since she came to London, and she felt more at ease than she had for ages. She had been feeling rather tired when she answered the phone, having spent all day translating articles in Spanish newspapers into English. At first, it had been stimulating and interesting, but after the afternoon stint from two o'clock till six she had a headache from concentrating so hard on getting the English translation right. They didn't want a literal version; it had to read well—and that was the really hard part because Irena was not a trained journalist and was learning as she went along. She had had to do each piece several times before she got it right.

She would have gone home an hour ago, but she had had to wait for Gina because it hadn't occurred to her to ask for a key to Gina's flat, so she couldn't have got in if she had gone back home alone.

When Gina came into the office a few minutes later she looked tired, too, her russet hair lacklustre and her green eyes dull.

Irena gave her a vivid smile. 'You just missed Daniel—Roz is doing very well now. She must be—Daniel is making jokes!'

Gina laughed, her weariness shed for that instant. 'Is he really? Oh, Irena, I'm so relieved, I haven't been able to concentrate on anything else since it happened.'

'I know, I've been the same. But she sends her love to you and she will ring you from the hospital as soon as the staff let her use a phone.'

'I expect she'll be phoning her story through before the day's out,' said Gina with amusement, 'if I know Roz!'

'Daniel said it was typical Amery fireworks,' Irena told her and they both laughed.

'You don't seem to have inherited them,' Gina said, studying Irena curiously.

She shook her head with a rueful look. 'No, I didn't—I can't see myself as a foreign correspondent. I get nervous just talking to strangers—this morning when I went down to get my sandwiches from the snack bar there was a young man in there, selling...' She paused, frowning, hesitating. 'Is it selling? Serving?'

'Serving,' Gina nodded. 'Was he Italian? Youngish? That would be Roberto Torelli. Don't tell me he wasn't friendly? He usually is!'

'Oh, he was friendly, but he kept staring, and he made me nervous! Roz would just shrug, but I cannot do that, I am...oh, what is the word? I feel silly.'

'Self-conscious?'

Irena sighed. 'Yes, that is the word. I am too conscious of myself with strangers; Roz never is.'

Gina considered her thoughtfully. 'Are you shy with women too—or is it just men?'

'More with men than women,' Irena admitted. 'It is the way I was brought up, I think. I lived on a farm, and went to school in the nearest little town. It is a remote part of Spain, and things have not changed there the way they have on the coast, where they get tourists.'

'London must be something of a culture shock, then!'

'Paris was,' Irena said, laughing suddenly. 'I came from my little village, wide-eyed and open-mouthed, and found myself surrounded with men all trying to date me!'

'Lucky old you,' said Gina, and both of them laughed, then Gina looked past Irena at the doorway and her face cooled. 'Oh, hello,' she said and Irena turned, knowing she would see Nick Caspian because Gina always took on that icy look when she saw him.

What she did not expect was to see Esteban with him—it was something of a shock to her. Her face stiffened, and she turned away again.

She still hadn't got over the contemptuous way Esteban had spoken to her and then kissed her, after he dragged her out of the photographic studio. She had barely seen him since, she had begun to wonder if he was avoiding her, if he was embarrassed—well, he should be, even if he wasn't! He had behaved badly, not just over that kiss—but jumping to all the wrong conclusions about her again.

She wasn't ready to accept apologies, this time. She could see a pattern in his behaviour. Esteban did not trust or probably even like women. He always thought the worst of them, and that explained the sense of brooding anger she had picked up in him the first time they met, on that plane. He had looked at her with dis-taste and icy remoteness because he thought she was trying to pick him up, and she felt a jab of angry shame because she couldn't deny she would have liked to meet him, she had been attracted to him.

That might be why Esteban had assumed that she was flirting with that photographer? Did he think she flirted with every man she met? Her skin burned at the very idea. Was that why he had kissed her in that brutal, contemptuous way?

'What was all that about you being surrounded by men trying to date you in Paris, Irena?' Nick Caspian asked in an amused voice.

Deeply aware of Esteban watching her, Irena stammered, 'Well, French men can be very...' She broke off, and Nick grinned.

'Amorous?'

'Romantic,' she hurriedly offered.

'French men like women, that's why they're so gorgeous!' said Gina.

Nick turned narrowed eyes on her. 'So that's why you were so keen on Paris! Did you meet any romantic Frenchmen?'

'One or two,' she said, her green eyes cold, and Nick scowled.

'If it's romantic to like women, most men are romantic!' He turned to the other man, as if for masculine support. 'What about Spaniards, Esteban? They're romantic, they like women, don't they?'

'In their place,' Esteban said offhandedly, and Gina stared at him, her green eyes opening wide.

'I don't believe I heard that! Did you hear what he said, Irena? What is our place, Esteban? The kitchen, I suppose?'

'A man's bed,' Nick drawled, laughing.

'Oh, you would say that!' Gina's hands screwed up into fists as if she would hit him and Nick stopped laughing, watching her.

'It was a joke, just a joke! No need to start a fight.'

'Except that you half mean it,' Gina threw at him, and he shrugged.

'If you're offering, you'd be welcome in my bed any time, yes!'

Irena's mouth opened in a silent gasp. She was startled, but oddly enough not surprised by what Nick had said. The two of them were always quarrelling, whenever she saw them together, yet she had begun to suspect that that was not what Nick wanted, that it was Gina who was antagonistic to him and Nick was merely reacting to her hostility.

Gina's hand flew up to hit him, and he blocked it effortlessly, catching her wrist and forcing her arm down again, staring into her eyes, his mouth hard.

'Don't even try it, Gina. Women may be a match for men in some areas, but if it comes to blows they haven't got a prayer, so they're wiser not to start a fight.'

She was flushed and furious. Pulling free, she turned on her heel and rushed out of the room, and Nick followed her. Irena was too stunned to move; she stared as they vanished, the door slamming behind them.

Esteban whistled softly under his breath. 'Those two are an explosion just waiting to happen!'

Irena gave him an indignant look. 'You started that quarrel!'

'I did?' His jet eyes stared. 'What are you talking about?'

'Your stupid remark about women being OK in their place! You offended Gina and Nick got the blame!'

'They would have had that row over something else if they had not had it over me! The two of them are so charged up they quarrel over anything and everything.' Esteban gave a cynical shrug, his face bleak. 'If they would just go to bed and get it over with they would stop being so on edge.'

Irena went pink, remembering that kiss, the way her mouth had felt afterwards, the new, unfamiliar ache inside her. Huskily, she said, 'Sex isn't the answer to everything!'

'Who said it was?' he muttered, frowning. 'It's the basic life instinct, though! Every animal feels the same drive.'

'We aren't animals!' she said, reverting instinctively to Spanish, the tongue in which she felt most able to argue without hesitation, and Esteban laughed shortly, answering her in Spanish, too.

'That's exactly what we are. Human beings are animals, and if we try to bury our instincts we're likely to have a problem sooner or later.'

'We were animals once, but we've had thousands of years of civilisation behind us since then,' Irena protested. 'Sex may be a basic human drive, but love is more powerful, not just between a man and a woman, but between a mother and her child, a father and a child!'

He laughed. 'I'm not getting into that argument! Men and women have spent centuries disagreeing over that.'

'And men have always been wrong,' she said, remembering his accusation the other day, and the way he had kissed her. 'About women's feelings, anyway. We simply don't react the way you do—and you're lucky my brothers haven't heard what you've just said to me! They would have got violent.'

'You have brothers, too? Older than you?'

'Younger. Ramón isn't quite eighteen, and Miguel is sixteen.'

Esteban's brows met and he looked rather puzzled. 'I didn't realise Des had sons of that age.'

Irena's colour rose and she lowered her eyes, not knowing what to say. She had never explained her true relationship to Des and Roz.

He stared at her as she hesitated. She hated to lie, even by evasion, so at last she told him the truth, huskily, a little shyly.

'They...they are not Des's children.' She took a breath and then plunged on, 'My mother was never his wife. She married a Spaniard while she was expecting me, which is why I grew up in Spain. Roz is my half-sister, Des was married to her mother, but she died before he met mine, and my mother felt that Des didn't really love her, he was still grieving for his dead wife, so she didn't tell him when she realised she was going to have a baby. She never told me about him, either, until my father...I mean, her husband, who I thought was my father, of course, died, and then she told me the truth. I was very upset, I didn't really believe her, and then I met Des in Paris a few months later, and he showed me a photo of his own mother, and I looked so like her that I realised it was all true.'

She stopped speaking abruptly, and couldn't risk meeting his eyes for fear of what she might see—pity, distaste, curiosity. She wanted none of those from him. Irena didn't know why Esteban's reactions should matter so much, she only knew that they did; that, for some reason she hadn't yet worked out, Esteban had the power to hurt, or make her happy, with a word or a look.

When he was silent, she broke out shakily, 'Oh, I shouldn't have told you! Des wouldn't want anyone to know. Please, don't repeat what I've told you to anyone!'

'I won't tell another living soul,' Esteban promised, then his hand caught hold of her chin and pushed her head back.

She felt her pulses beating like flames in a high wind and was afraid of meeting his eyes, her own flickering away, nervous and uneasy.

'You can trust me, Irena,' he murmured. 'I swear I'll never tell anyone what you just told me.'

She risked a look at him, her enormous grey eyes searching his face. 'I want to trust you, but...'

'You can,' he insisted.

'How can I when I never know where I am with you?' she broke out. 'One minute you're kind, the next you turn nasty, the way you did when you dragged me out of that photographer's studio and...'

She could not mention the kiss, not even by implication, but Esteban knew what she meant. A dark colour grew in his face, his jet eyes glittered and his mouth was a grim line.

'That's how you looked then!' she muttered. 'You insulted me, saying that I'd wanted... him to... to touch me! Some girls may enjoy that sort of experience, but I don't!'

'You should never have let him maul you about the way he did.'

'I told him not to touch me like that, but he didn't take any notice!'

'You should have walked out!'

'I should have slapped you round the face when you kissed me, too!' she threw back, her face hot.

There was a silence and she felt her ears drumming with alarm, then Esteban said in a clipped voice, 'Yes, you should! I apologise for that, I was in a temper, but I had no business taking it out on you.'

She felt even worse then, close to tears. 'I only went to the picture desk editor to get snapshots for my security pass! I don't know why that photographer was taking that sort of picture of me!'

'I can tell you,' Esteban said flatly. 'Tim Doyle, the picture editor, thought you would look good on the *Sentinel* calendar.'

Her face was blank. 'What?'

He grimaced, his voice sardonic. 'Oh, it's one of Nick Caspian's new projects! He is running a sort of beauty contest in the paper, using pictures of girls sent in by readers, mostly in bikinis or very sexy outfits, and the calendar will be a spin-off from it.' Esteban paused and shrugged wryly. 'It's a brilliant marketing device, of course. Everyone who has sent in a picture of his daughter or girlfriend, or wife, will want to buy the calendar to see if she is in it. That's the theory, anyway, and Nick's marketing theories are usually only too accurate.'

Irena stared at him with a puzzled expression. 'But if the pictures have all been sent in by readers, why did the picture editor want a photo of me?'

'He was planning to plant a picture of you among the others.'

She still did not understand. 'But why?'

'Oh, it's strictly against the rules, but it is done quite often on some papers—they plant letters when their postbag isn't up to much, and it's typical of the picture editor, always looking for the better angle. Tim Doyle thought all the snaps that had come in were much the same, and he wanted something different. When you walked in, he had the idea of using you, instead of a professional model. It would be hard to prove it was a plant, you see.'

Irena looked horrified. 'Oh, but I don't want to have my picture in the *Sentinel*, or on this calendar, especially looking like that!'

Esteban's mouth twisted. 'You don't have to worry about it, they won't use you. I've made it quite clear that they're not to come within ten feet of you again, too.' He gave her a wry smile. 'It can be useful sometimes to be head of marketing, you see.'

Irena smiled back, then asked, 'Sorry to be stupid, but exactly what does that mean? Head of marketing? I've been meaning to ask—are you in charge of selling the newspaper?'

'No, that's the sales manager's job. I sell everything but the newspaper.'

She still didn't understand. 'Oh, I see. I think.'

Esteban patiently explained further, 'Look, there are all sorts of merchandising spin-offs from the *Sentinel*, from T-shirts to books and records, even videos, and, of course, this calendar. It's my job to come up with ideas for new products, and then see that they're produced at the right price, and that *Sentinel* readers want to buy them. That's very important, of course— we create the market for our own products, so we have to pitch the price at exactly what we think people will pay. If the price is too high, they won't buy, and oddly enough it can be just as dangerous to put too low a price on something. People are wary of it, then, and think there must be something wrong with it. You have to be clever enough to guess what they think something is worth.'

'It sounds like a very interesting job,' Irena said. 'Thank you for explaining to me—and for clearing up the mystery about the photographer. I thought he was a little crazy.'

'Not at all,' Esteban said gravely. 'He was just following orders.'

She nodded. 'Well, thank you—and thank you for promising not to talk about—about what I told you.'

'I wouldn't have done, anyway,' he assured her. 'I have a fellow feeling for Des. I have had painful experiences which I find hard to talk about.'

'What——?' she began, and then broke off, biting her lower lip as she saw his face darken. 'No, sorry, forget I asked...'

They heard voices outside the office at that instant. Nick and Gina were returning. Esteban glanced over his shoulder, then said quickly, 'Will you have dinner with me tonight, Irena?'

The door opened before she could answer and Gina said ruefully, 'Sorry to keep you hanging around, Irena— you must be starving, it is almost dinner time and you have been waiting all this time. Shall we go home first and change, or just go down to Pierre's and eat first?'

Irena gave Esteban an uncertain glance, her grey eyes shy. 'Well, actually, Gina, I...we...'

'I had just asked Irena to have dinner with me, Gina,' Esteban finished for her when she broke off, stammering.

'Oh,' Gina said, startled, giving him an interested look.

Drily, Nick murmured, 'Shall we make a foursome of it, then?'

Esteban frowned and Gina, watching him, said quickly, 'No, sorry, I have other things to do this evening. I have to get home as soon as possible. Irena, I'll give you a key so that you can come back to the flat whenever

you like.' She produced a spare key and gave it to Irena.
'See you later. Enjoy your evening out, and forget about
Roz for a while!' and then Gina collected up her things,
and left, with Nick sauntering after her.

'Have fun, you two,' he drawled over his shoulder,
and Irena's flush deepened.

'Are we going to have dinner in Pierre's?' she asked
Esteban to cover her confusion, but he shook his head.

'No, I thought I would show you something of London
tonight, so we'll be taking a drive, and then maybe you
would like to be reminded of home. I know a Spanish
restaurant in Hampstead—what do you think? Would
you like some Spanish food?'

'I'd love some, it's ages since I ate real Spanish food.
In Paris they cook paella, but it doesn't taste the same,
it is too bland.'

'This restaurant has a Spanish cook, it is a family
place—the wife runs the tables and the husband is in the
kitchen, cooking. He is from my own part of Spain...
Castile...near Segovia...and you know what they say
about our weather. Nine months of winter and three
months of hell! You either freeze in a bitter wind, or
burn under a terrible sun. It isn't a country that breeds
soft men. Juan is a traditional cook, you won't get any
bland paella from him. He uses spices to take your breath
away and a lot of garlic and onions.'

Irena laughed. 'I love lots of spices and garlic.'

'Just as well!' Esteban was looking almost light-
hearted. Now she knew he came from the harsh mountains of old Castile she understood him far more.
Andalucía was quite a mild climate, by comparison. They
had bad winters, in her own mountains, but they were
above the mild Mediterranean coast and didn't suffer as

badly as they could do in Castile, whose nearest coastline edged the stormtorn Bay of Biscay.

'I must ring Juan before we leave,' he said, picking up the phone, and she watched him secretly, from behind her lashes, while he made his call. Now she understood his harshness, his strength, his brooding anger. His nature reflected the landscape in which he had grown up; undoubtedly he had learnt to be an autocratic male, as had her brothers, expecting to dominate and domineer over the women in their lives.

They took the lift down to the underground car park and drove out into North Street, then turned into Silver Street, following the square of the Barbary Wharf complex to turn at last into Ratcliff Walk and drive along by the river towards the ancient stone walls of the Tower of London, dreaming gently in the evening sunlight, as if they had never been a terror and a threat to the people of London, never seen prisoners marched through those great gates, or beheaded on the smooth green turf within.

The City of London proper lay just beyond the Tower. During the day, as Irena had discovered, it was crammed with people all hurrying to and fro, but now it was a different place; all the banks, offices and financial institutions were closed for the night, their staff gone home and the streets well nigh deserted.

Esteban turned north from there and soon they were out of the centre of London, driving up quite steep hills through streets of large Victorian houses. Esteban drove a sports car, a Ferrari—small but powerful, it nipped through the traffic like a cat, suddenly streaking ahead whenever there was a chance.

'This is Hampstead,' he said, his brown hands relaxed on the wheel as they were stopped by a red light. 'The heath itself is at the far end of this street; we'll take a look at it before we go to Juan's place.'

He parked the car in a side-street near the heath, and they got out and walked over the grass, under the trees. The darkness was falling now, but there were still plenty of people out.

It was a short walk, but Irena got the feeling of the place, the ambience: they were high up, above London's close-set houses. The sky arched above them, a few stars came out and moonlight glimmered behind a cloud somewhere, reflected in a pond they passed. They saw men walking dogs, women with children playing ball, joggers in running gear, girls in short skirts who had been playing tennis, and people flying kites who were just beginning to wind up the string and put their kites away.

'So many people doing so many different things,' Irena thought aloud. 'It is lovely here. It must be a nice place to live.'

Around the heath stood more of those large, gabled Victorian houses, their windows beginning to show lights as night set in across Hampstead.

'City life is strange, isn't it?' Esteban said as he and Irena stood and watched the street lamps gleaming through the branches of trees. They were speaking Spanish all the time; they had lapsed into it as soon as they were alone with a sense of relief and pleasure. 'A very artificial way of living, easier and softer than life in my village.'

'And mine!' she said ruefully. 'It was a hard life, we weren't rich, but we were always happy, I wouldn't have changed the way we lived, for anything—I wouldn't have wanted to grow up in a big city instead.'

'Nor would I,' he agreed.

She hesitated, then confessed, 'When I first got to London and found out that Roz was on that plane, and in such danger, I kept wishing I was back home.'

'Your mother still lives there, with your brothers?'

She nodded. 'Ramón and Miguel work the farm with her. It makes enough to live on. I go back there in the holidays—I love it there. It took me ages to get used to the noise of traffic all night, in Paris, and London is as bad. Cities are such noisy places. You can't hear yourself think, let alone get to sleep. At times I yearn to have a little silence!'

'I know what you mean,' he said. 'That was something my wife could never get used to, either, the noisiness of city life.'

Irena felt a jolt of pain, her grey eyes widened in shock. 'You . . . you're married?'

# CHAPTER SEVEN

ESTEBAN stood very still, not looking at Irena now, staring across the heath, his face harsh in profile, a carved stone statue except for the glitter of his eyes in the gathering dusk.

'I was married,' he said, 'She died.'

'Oh . . . I'm sorry . . .' Irena stammered.

He turned on his heel, his manner somehow rejecting her sympathy and even, she felt, her interest, as if to make her realise that she had no right to feel either. 'Shall we go and eat now? Juan's place is only a short walk, down the hill. We'll leave the car here, as it is difficult to park in Hampstead Village.'

She hurried after his long strides, her mind churning with questions she knew she would never dare ask after the curt way he had told her his wife had died. It was obvious that because they were speaking Spanish and he was relaxed he had blurted out that remark about his wife, and then regretted mentioning her. Esteban had pulled down the shutters again. She should have remembered his inbred pride; that Spanish legacy they were both heir to and found hard to shake off.

The more she learnt about him the more complex she realised he must be—and the deeper her feelings about him went. He was beginning to haunt her mind, even when he wasn't there, she couldn't stop thinking about him.

Did anybody else at the *Sentinel* know that he had been married? Gina and Hazel certainly didn't, or they would surely have mentioned it—and if neither of them knew it wasn't likely that anybody else on the paper did, which meant that his wife must have died before he came to London.

How long ago had she died? wondered Irena, following him down the steep village street and round a corner into Hampstead High Street. Esteban's sensitivity might mean that she hadn't died very long ago— perhaps it was her death that had made him leave Spain to come to England?

'It isn't far now,' he muttered to her as they turned up a side-street leading off the High Street. The other shops were closed by then, but Irena knew where they were going, because she immediately saw an old black iron Spanish lamp hanging above a lighted bay window.

As they reached the door she saw another telltale sign—on the wall beside it a delicately painted china plaque in blue and yellow, bearing an image of the Madonna and Child with the name 'Juan's Place' painted below that. These plaques were very popular in Spain; you saw them beside front doors everywhere, carrying the name of the house and often a painting of the Virgin or a favourite saint. Sometimes, too, they were used as a holy water stoup, beside a statue of the Virgin, inside the front door, so that visitors could acquire a blessing by taking holy water before they entered the home.

Esteban pushed open the door and a bell rang. He stood back to let Irena pass him, and as she entered a short, black-haired man hurried towards her, his smile polite until he saw Esteban, when it broadened at once.

'Esteban!'

The two men shook hands and embraced at the same time, talking away to each other in deep, colloquial Spanish.

'I was just talking about you to my brother, on the phone—Jaime, you met him at that big game in Madrid last year, remember?' Juan said.

'Of course, how is he? That was an exciting game, he played well.'

Juan groaned. 'They lost three-two! I could have spat teeth. Exciting, you call it? I wouldn't like to say what I call it. They almost got that third goal; if the whistle hadn't gone just at the wrong moment, they'd have drawn, at least.'

Esteban nodded. 'And if Corbus hadn't sprained that ankle they would have won!'

'He's always been prone to leg problems. He pulled a calf muscle last season, and was out of the game for weeks,' Juan said, sighing. 'He's getting old. We all are, even you, Esteban! I found a grey hair the other day. Don't tell Lidia, she'll start trying to get me to dye it.'

Esteban grinned. 'How is Lidia? Isn't she here tonight?'

'Sure, she'll be out any minute. She just went out into the yard to cut some chives and basil—we grow our own.' Juan's dark eyes turned with polite interest towards Irena and Esteban introduced her.

'Irena, this is my old friend, Juan Martino. Juan, this is Irena Olivero.'

'A nice Spanish girl, at last! We were afraid he would date nothing but English girls,' Juan said, his grin wicked.

'His idea of a joke, take no notice!' Esteban said.

Juan formally kissed Irena's hand. 'Welcome to our place, Irena—I may call you Irena, I hope?'

'Of course,' she said, furious with herself for blushing like a teenager. When would she stop doing that? It was so embarrassing; what must Juan think of her?

'And you must call me Juan! What are you doing in London?' Juan ran a speculative eye over her. 'Let me guess! You're a student!'

'Yes...' she admitted, laughing.

'Lucky devil, Esteban! Beautiful and clever, and barely out of the cradle!' Juan roared with laughter, but Esteban wasn't so amused. His face had tightened, his brows met.

Juan saw that, too, and said hurriedly, 'Only a joke, old boy, only my stupid idea of a joke again! You know my sense of humour. Quite tasteless. I envy you, like crazy, take no notice of me.' Then he asked Irena, 'What are you studying? English?'

She shook her head. 'I'm just working in London for the vacation, translating on the *Sentinel*. I'm actually studying French at the Sorbonne, in Paris.'

Juan looked interested. 'Planning a career in hotels? Languages can be very useful. If you ever want a job in a restaurant, I'll be glad to give you a try.'

'She doesn't need a job as a waitress, Juan. She is paid very well on the *Sentinel*,' Esteban said, steering her into the restaurant. 'Where shall we sit?'

'Where you please,' said Juan. 'Irena, what will you have to drink?'

'Just a little wine,' she said as Esteban chose a table and pulled out a chair for her.

'*Blanco, dulce, espumoso, rosado, seco, tinto*?' recited Juan.

'Stop showing off!' Esteban smiled at her. 'Which do you want?'

'White wine, please.'

'*Blanco*, for Irena, then, and I think I'll drink dry white wine myself. And we'll go on to red later with the main course, if we feel like it.'

Juan vanished and came back with a carafe of wine; he poured each of them a glass and left the copper carafe on the table, then returned a moment later with a tray of tiny dishes which he placed in the middle of the table, too.

'*Tapas y entreméses*,' he said. 'Eat and enjoy!' Then a dark-haired woman came into the restaurant from the kitchen to put some more small dishes on the bar and Juan looked around. 'Ah, here's Lidia! Darling, he's here, come and say hello!'

'Esteban! My favourite man! Wonderful to see you!' She came over to give him a kiss, and then shook hands with Irena, studying her with as much interest as her husband had a few minutes earlier. 'So, you're Spanish? How long have you been over here? Your English is good! Better than mine!'

'You don't work at it,' teased her husband.

'When do I have time? I use it every day, serving customers, I get by.' She grinned at Irena. 'The clients want to hear me speak English with plenty of Spanish accent; they prefer it, anyway!'

'Because you're a woman, and very sexy,' said Juan, pretending to be jealous and sulky. 'They fancy you—and you love it!'

She pinched his cheek. 'Don't be a naughty boy!' They were obviously happy together, they smiled like lovers. Lidia was in her thirties, not pretty, but very attractive, with smooth golden skin and big dark eyes, a very rounded body and a warm smile.

'I suppose I'd better get into the kitchen and start cooking,' Juan said, looking at his watch. 'See you later, you two! Don't go without saying goodbye, will you?'

Lidia tied on a white apron, and handed them each a menu. 'Eat your *tapas*!' she urged, and Irena looked at the little saucers of food—each was different but all looked delicious to her. She hadn't eaten *tapas* for months.

There was whitebait, mushrooms in a tomato sauce, squid cooked with garlic, small slices of spicy sausage, halves of hard-boiled egg stuffed with a mayonnaise mixture.

'If we eat too many of these, I won't want anything else,' Esteban said drily.

'We must at least taste some or Lidia will be insulted,' Irena said, watching the older woman greeting some newcomers and showing them to a table.

Esteban used the provided small fork to pick up some sausage and ate it while they sipped their wine and looked at the menu. Irena absently tasted a few of the *tapas*, too, while she decided on her own meal—*caldo de pescado*, a fish soup, for a starter, then an Asturian white-bean dish which her mother had often cooked. Just seeing it on the menu made her very homesick. Esteban started with grilled prawns and then a very colourful dish of chicken cooked with red peppers and tomatoes served on saffron rice.

'No paella, then?' he said as Irena ordered her meal, and she laughed and shook her head, explaining why she had chosen the white-bean dish.

'I hope Juan makes it the way your mother did!' Lidia said ruefully, because there were many ways of making the bean dish, just as there were a thousand different varieties of paella, each a regional speciality. Lidia and Esteban discussed which Rioja was the best in the house, then she glanced at the *tapas* saucers. 'What did you think of the squid? One of my best *tapas*.'

'Delicious,' they both agreed.

'And I loved the sauce you cooked the mushrooms in!' Irena told her, which made Lidia smile with pleasure.

'A recipe of my grandmother. Don't ask what's in it, it's a closely guarded family secret.'

Some more clients arrived, the restaurant was filling up now, and Lidia became very busy. A few minutes later she served them their first course and brought the Rioja in a wicker basket, leaving it open to breathe until they were ready to start on it, when they moved on to their second course.

Irena's white-bean dish was superb; strongly flavoured with garlic just as her mother made it. They made small talk uneasily over the meal; Irena was grateful for the long silences while they ate.

'You worked in Madrid before you came here?' she asked politely, and he nodded. 'I've only been there once, on a day-trip, on a coach.'

'You must go again! It's one of the loveliest cities in the world—the architecture is magnificent. I was very happy there for years.' He paused and stared down into his glass of red wine.

'Are you planning to go back there one day, as you were so happy?' she asked uncertainly, not sure how far to go in asking questions.

He shook his head, his face sombre, took another long swallow of wine. 'I stopped being happy after Dominga died.'

'Your wife?' she tentatively whispered.

He nodded, tracing a line up and down the stem of his glass with one fingertip.

There was a silence, then he muttered, 'She was only twenty, no age at all. It was my fault she died like that. An accident—she fell down stairs.'

Irena drew a startled breath. 'Oh, how terrible!'

'The fall didn't kill her,' he said, 'But she was going to have a baby, and something went wrong, because of the fall—and she died. I wasn't even there.' His voice was bitter. 'I was never there, I was so busy, I was in my first important job and I had to keep going away, leaving her alone for days on end. She missed her mother, she had no friends in Madrid. She was lonely.'

'How did you meet her?' whispered Irena.

'She came from my village in Castile—I'd known her since she was born, her brother was my best friend at school, Bernardo. We were seven years old when Dominga was born, the first girl in his family; his mother was so happy. She had five boys and had been lighting candles to the Virgin, praying for a girl. Dominga was the answer to her prayer—she was beautiful, too, even as a little girl. From the beginning I decided to marry her. I told everyone—"I'm going to marry Dominga when I'm grown up". Bernardo liked the idea; he wanted me for a brother-in-law.'

Irena smiled, touched by the picture of the two little boys planning their future as brothers-in-law. 'When did you ask Dominga?'

'On and off while she was growing up. I formally proposed to her as soon as she left school. She was sixteen, her mother thought that was much too young, and she was right, of course. She made us wait until Dominga was eighteen.'

Irena worked it out in her head—if his wife had been eighteen, he must only have been twenty-five himself. He kept talking about how young Dominga had been, but Esteban had been young, too. Much too young to know how to cope with that terrible trauma; losing someone you loved was always hard, but it was more difficult when you were young and had no experience of such loss, especially if you felt guilty about it, too.

Esteban drank some more wine and refilled his glass. Irena had barely touched her own glass and shook her head when he looked at her to see if she wanted some more.

'She was still too young,' he muttered into his glass.

'Spanish girls do marry young,' argued Irena, wondering if he needed to reproach himself because it was the only way he could cope with his guilt.

Lidia came and cleared their plates, asked if they wanted a dessert.

'*Higos*?' she suggested when they couldn't think of what they wanted, and they both nodded, agreeing that fresh figs would be the perfect ending for the rather heavy meal they had eaten.

When Lidia went off to get the figs, Irena asked, 'Did your wife have a job in Madrid?'

'She worked at home, making clothes—she wasn't clever, but she could sew beautifully; the nuns had taught her to make lace by hand, and embroider. She made expensive clothes by hand, for sale in the Madrid boutiques. She was well paid, they were very sought after. But it meant that she worked alone, at home. That first year we were very happy, though. Then I got promotion, and my job took up more and more of my time, and sometimes Dominga went home to stay with her family, and we started quarrelling. She was too young to be away from them.'

'You were both too young,' Irena said gently.

He looked at her with bleak, dark eyes. 'I was about five years older than you are now!'

'Four,' she protested.

His eyes were wry. 'You aren't twenty-one yet!'

'Of course I am,' she said, pink; and he smiled briefly, his eyes warming to her until the shadow fell on his face again.

'Dominga was twenty when she got pregnant—we'd been married two years, but we had agreed not to have a baby for a while, because we were still quite poor. She knew I didn't want to start a family yet. I think she planned the baby, deliberately, to try to keep me at home, but if so it didn't work out that way. I was shocked when she told me, I was even angry, because I was scared— we were managing quite well but our flat was rented, and we had to be careful with money. It started another bitter quarrel, just when she needed my support.' He ran a hand over his face, as if trying to wipe off the guilt he felt. 'I was a selfish bastard.'

Irena didn't know what to say, she watched him help-lessly. He was suffering so much, but what did you say to a man carrying that much guilt? She felt inadequate.

After a moment he went on flatly, 'From then on, I worked even harder, because we would need more money when the baby arrived. Dominga was six months pregnant when I was sent to America for a month by Caspian International, to study American marketing techniques. She could have come, but she wouldn't. She was afraid of flying, she was a very highly strung girl, and she was lost enough in Madrid; she couldn't face the idea of going to New York. And she was nervous about the baby coming early, the travelling seemed too much of a strain. So she stayed at home, and while I was in New York she had the accident; she lost the baby and...' He broke off, his face grim. 'I flew back at once, of course, but she was dead before I got there. Her family never spoke to me again. They blamed me, and they didn't want me at the funeral. They buried her in the family plot, back in the village. They wouldn't have me in the house. At the funeral, they all ignored me. Her mother never got over it. Dominga was her favourite child, her only daughter, and I haven't seen Bernardo since. He felt it was his fault for having wanted her to marry me.'

'That was very unfair!' Irena protested. 'It wasn't your fault—you couldn't have been with her all day long, even if you had stayed in your village and worked on the land! She could have had that accident anywhere, any time, and it wouldn't have been your fault.'

'I married her and took her away from her family, and that made her unhappy. So it was my fault,' Esteban said flatly, his face stubborn.

Why had he told her all this? she wondered, falling silent as she realised the futility of arguing with him. Esteban had lived with the guilt for so long that it was second nature to him; he wouldn't relinquish it easily.

And it explained so much—his brooding air, his inner anger with himself, with fate, with life; his remoteness and his sudden hunger, the day he'd kissed her with such force and demand.

They ate their figs, sprinkled with roast split almonds and floating in cream, and then Lidia brought them strong coffee and pieces of Turrón de Jijona, little squares of soft nougat made with honey, nuts and cinnamon, which Irena had not tasted for years.

'I make them myself,' Lidia said. 'They're quite easy—I'll tell you how to make them some time. Excuse me, that young couple are looking bad-tempered; Juan is taking a long time cooking their duck.'

Irena looked at her watch as Lidia hurried away. 'Good heavens, look at the time! I must go soon, or I won't be fit for work tomorrow morning.'

'How are you enjoying it on the foreign desk?'

'Very much, it's fascinating to watch them work, and I'm enjoying my translating, but it is very tiring, having to concentrate so hard.'

'I'm sure it must be, but think how much English you're learning. It was a very good idea to come over here. I suppose you've worked on the Caspian paper in Paris?'

She nodded. 'During the Easter vacation Des got me a job there, and that was tough enough. But my French is much, much better than my English.'

'Your English is coming along nicely,' Esteban said kindly, smiling at her, and she felt her heart turn over.

When he looked like that he was devastating, and she wished he would always be so nice, that that black shadow would not fall over him again, he would not withdraw into the icy wasteland of his memories, of his guilt over his dead wife.

Lidia came over to their table to ask, 'Well, did you enjoy your meal?' and they thanked her again, praised Juan's cooking.

'You must go and say goodbye to him, Esteban,' Lidia said. 'He wants a word alone with you; we so rarely see you. Irena, let me give you some more coffee, everyone has had their main course and my girl can serve their desserts from the trolley while I sit with you and have a chat.'

Esteban obediently went off to the kitchen, smiling at Irena as he went, and Lidia got herself another cup and saucer and poured herself some coffee before sitting down at the table opposite Irena.

'So, tell me about yourself—where do you come from?'

Irena told her about the farm, her mother and brothers, the Andalucían mountains and the busy chaos of the coast below—and Lidia talked about her own home town, which was near Barcelona.

'Esteban and Juan grew up in the same village, though,' she said, giving Irena a serious look. 'I couldn't help overhearing, by the way, Esteban telling you about Dominga... it was a very sad thing to happen, but it was years ago, seven or eight years, I think, and he should have got over it by now. It was hardly his fault she had the accident while he was away, but Esteban took all the blame, and Juan says her family behaved very badly.'

'It sounded that way to me,' Irena ventured uncertainly, not sure she should discuss Esteban's private life behind his back. She didn't think he would like it if he ever found out.

'She was very spoilt,' Lidia said, leaning closer and lowering her voice. 'An only girl, with all these doting brothers, and doting parents, too—she was lovely, that was the trouble, and she couldn't accept real life after growing up like a little princess. She wanted Esteban to spoil her and pet her all the time, the way her family had, she couldn't understand that he had to work, she wanted him there all the time.'

'Maybe she would have grown up in the end, once she had a child herself,' suggested Irena, and Lidia nodded, then her eyes flicked to the kitchen doorway and she got up.

'Here's Esteban back, I'd better get on with my work too. Nice to have met you, Irena. I hope we see you again, often.'

They took a taxi back to the city, in the end, since Esteban decided he had drunk rather too much of the wine and he didn't want to risk driving his own car.

'I'll pick it up early tomorrow morning,' he shrugged. 'It will be OK where I parked it, overnight.'

He insisted on seeing her inside the flats, walked her to the lift and said goodnight.

Irena murmured huskily, 'Thank you for a very pleasant evening, I liked your friends, and it was wonderful to eat real Spanish food again. Juan is a great cook.'

He looked down at her, smiling. 'I'm glad you enjoyed it.'

That smile went to her head again. She stood on tiptoe, on impulse, and kissed his cheek.

Esteban looked startled for a second, taken off guard, his jet eyes glittered fiercely, then his hands caught her face, framed it between them, and he bent, his mouth searching for hers. Irena swayed closer, her arms going round his neck, clinging to him like a vine to a strong tree. Her lips parted softly, her eyes closed. The kiss made her tremble, her heartbeats shaking her whole body. The first time he kissed her had distressed her. This time she met his mouth, quivering with passion, and the kiss lasted much longer.

It was Esteban who ended it, pulling back with a sound like a groan. 'No! I can't,' he ground out between his teeth, looking down at her flushed and drowsy face with eyes that ate it. 'No, Irena—can't you see, it's impossible? I could never love anyone else, I have no right to... Why do you think I told you about Dominga? You must see how hopeless it is...'

Then he pushed her away and strode across the lobby out into the night while she stared after him, her face stricken.

# CHAPTER EIGHT

HAZEL'S wedding-day was sunny, but windy; as she got out of the limousine bringing her and her father to church her veil blew up to reveal her face and her skirts whisked around her like meringue. One of the photographers, who was making a video of the wedding for them as a wedding present, rushed in to capture the moment, grinning. As she saw him, Hazel began to laugh, clutching her veil with one hand and her wedding bouquet with the other, but by the time she was walking down the aisle on her father's arm her mood had swung round again, and she was quivering with tears.

Her father looked down at her, horrified. 'What's wrong, darling?'

'I'm so happy,' Hazel choked.

Her father laughed, relieved. 'Oh, is that all? You're a funny girl sometimes—I thought you were ill!'

She was just so strung up that she laughed and cried over nothing at all. She had never been so tense or so happy in her life.

Ahead of her Piet waited, elegant in morning dress, the sunlight filtering through the church's stained-glass windows gleaming on his well-brushed blond hair. Nick Caspian was best man, a little taller than Piet, dark where he was fair, leaner and more muscled—but Hazel barely noticed Nick, she was looking at Piet with her heart in her eyes. She had spent months planning this day, and now it was here the emotion fountained inside her almost unbearably. The music swelled in triumph, the congregation turned to look at her, smiling, their familiar faces a blur to her as she passed, her veil still down over her face, hiding her tears.

Roz was one of her bridesmaids and thank heavens she had no need of a wheelchair, she would walk on her own two legs. Her pretty blue dress, almost the same colour as her eyes, had a deep shawl collar which hid the strapping over her shoulder wound, although the short sleeves left bare the square dressing on her upper arm. She was paler than usual, and visibly much thinner, but apart from those reminders of the hijacking she looked almost normal.

Only Daniel knew that Roz was having nightmares; that although the physical scars were healing well there were unseen scars which were taking longer to fade.

'It's stupid,' she had said to him last night, waking in tears from a terrifying dream and clinging to him like a scared child. 'I'm more frightened now than I was at the time!'

He had held her close, murmuring soothingly. 'It's quite normal, darling. At the time you were using up your adrenalin, the old fight or flight stuff—you were scared, but we can always put up with far more than we ever think we can if we have to! But now that you're safe your nerves are playing up in your sleep.'

'How long is it going on, though?' she had said, white and haggard, and Daniel had held her even tighter, kissing her hair.

'It will pass, darling. Give yourself time, be patient—it only happened a couple of weeks ago! After the wedding, we'll go away for this holiday Nick has offered us. Made up your mind yet where you want to go?'

She hadn't, and they whiled away an hour talking about that. Roz knew Daniel was trying to take her mind off her nightmare, trying to change the colour of her mood, and he succeeded. When they fell asleep again she had no more bad dreams.

Daniel wanted to go to the West Indies or Mauritius, but as she watched Hazel and Piet making their vows in that gentle English sunlight Roz suddenly knew that she wanted to spend some time in the English countryside, not go back to hot suns and brilliant blue seas. While she was in that oven of a plane with the heat haze dancing on the horizon and sweat trickling down her back, making her clothes stick to her overheated skin, she had been thinking all the time of green fields and cool skies, the sound of water running between ferny banks, the smell of grass and English rain. That was what she wanted now: a little peace, a lazy week or two doing nothing much in those surroundings.

She told Daniel during the reception, watching him uncertainly. 'Do you mind, not getting some sun?'

He shook his head, his dark eyes full of love. 'It sounds perfect to me. Where shall we go? A hotel in the West Country?'

'No, I don't want to stay in a busy hotel. I want somewhere quiet. Maybe we could rent a cottage somewhere remote—we'll look into it tomorrow,' Roz said.

Nick had overheard something of what they were saying. Turning their way, his elbow on the white-clothed table, he interrupted quietly, 'My mother has a little house just outside Lyme Regis, Roz—if you're interested. The last tenant moved out two weeks ago, my mother is thinking of selling it so she hasn't let it again—at the moment it is empty. You can have it rent-free for as long as you like. There are no neighbours, it sits in a walled garden, down a narrow lane a few minutes from the sea, but there are shops and a pub just a short walk away.'

Daniel and Roz exchanged looks. 'That's very kind of you, Nick,' Roz said, slowly, taken aback by the unexpected offer. 'Are you sure your mother wouldn't mind?'

He shook his head. 'She will be only too pleased, when I tell her. She has heard all about your exploits, and she's full of admiration for you, she followed the hijacking story on the TV news.' He grinned. 'She's one of your father's fans, too!'

'Aren't we all?' Roz said, laughing, then sobered. 'I only wish I knew where he was right now. We still haven't heard a squeak out of him—I suppose he is *in* Vietnam?'

'He's there somewhere,' Nick assured her. 'But he presumably isn't ready to file copy yet. Sooner or later he'll surface.' He gave her a kind look. 'Do I have to tell you not to worry about him? I'm sure I don't. You know what Des is like, none better! He plays the game by his own rules, and we have to accept that if we want him to write for us.'

She sighed. 'True. Well, thanks for the offer of the house, anyway. I had no idea your mother had a house in England.'

'She hasn't used it for years. I look after it for her, or, rather, my staff do. As I say, it was let to good tenants. She kept it because she was attached to the place, and kept meaning to fly over here for a long visit, but she doesn't travel much now; she finds it too tiring. That is why she has decided at last to sell it, she says she isn't likely to use it any more, so why keep it?'

It must be nice to be so rich that you can keep a house for years just in case you might want to use it one day, thought Roz drily, but that, of course, was not something she would risk saying to Nick Caspian. He was sometimes very democratic, talking to the cleaners or the typists on a chatty, casual level, as if he were one of them, but nobody made the mistake of going too far with him. Under that friendly smile there was hard, cold steel which could as easily cut you into little pieces.

Nick frowned thoughtfully. 'By the way, while you're there, I'm afraid the local estate agent may bring buyers round to see it—that won't be a problem, will it?'

Roz hesitated. 'No, of course not,' she said, but she was wondering if she was up to keeping the house immaculate all the time while they were there, as would be necessary if people kept coming to view it.

Nick watched her, his sharp grey eyes shrewd. 'Don't let it worry you. No need for you and Daniel to be there when the agent comes with a client, of course, and did I say that we pay a cleaner to come in several times a week? She'll do all the housework for you, Roz; I wouldn't want you to lift so much as a duster. She can cook for you, too, if you like. She is a very nice woman, Mrs Petty. But I don't want to pressure you into accepting if it really isn't what you want. This is your holiday. Think about it, talk it over with Daniel, and let me know in your own good time.'

'That's very kind...thank you,' Roz murmured, and Daniel made agreeing noises.

Gina had listened to their conversation while she ate her smoked salmon and caviare, followed by a cold slice of game pie with a tossed green salad and then strawberries and cream. For once Nick seemed oblivious to her, his face in crisp profile, hard and clear as a new-minted coin, and she could look at him without being afraid he would turn and stare back. He was a baffling mixture. A hard man, full of drive and energy, fiercely competitive, one minute—and then he would do an apparent volte-face and become thoughtful, impulsively generous, kind. It was as if there were two personalities inside his skin. Jekyll and Hyde, she thought, smiling to herself!

'Share the joke with the rest of us, Gina!' Nick said, suddenly turning his head to catch that smile, and she met his eyes with a jolt of shock.

'Oh, it was nothing.' She felt a twinge of gratitude because he couldn't see inside her head. She didn't think he would be much amused by her flights of fancy.

Nick's narrowed eyes searched her face. 'That's the first sign, you know!'

'What is?'

'Laughing over nothing! Little men in white coats will come and take you away soon.'

She dropped her lashes over her eyes. 'Ha, ha.' Time to change the subject, she decided. 'It has been a beautiful wedding, hasn't it?'

'Has it made you want to have one of your own?' Nick drawled and a little flush crept into her face.

'You forget, I've been married!'

'That was enough for you, was it? You wouldn't care to try again?'

'Not at the moment, thanks,' she said with pretended lightness, forcing a light laugh.

He was watching her like a ferret watching a rabbit hole: suspecting there might be something down there and poised to find out.

'Wasn't your first marriage a happy experience, Gina? Is that why you're not keen on risking it again?'

'I was very happy!' Gina snapped, her green eyes hostile, but at that moment everyone began clapping and whistling, and they both looked round in surprise to see that Hazel and Piet were on their feet.

'They're going to cut the cake,' Nick said, and Gina shifted her chair so that she could watch as bride and groom picked up the large ceremonial knife to cut the three-tiered wedding cake. As they did so a number of photographers, amateur and professional, took pictures by flashlight, and the video cameraman moved around them with his camera mounted on his shoulder.

'There are so many rituals to weddings,' Gina said wryly to Roz, who nodded.

'I suppose there are, it hadn't occurred to me before, but you're right—what a traditional lot we are.' Roz looked across the table at Irena, who had been very quiet during the reception lunch. 'Do they have as many rituals at a Spanish wedding, Irena?'

Irena shyly nodded. 'Just as many, if not more.' Spain was still a country rich with ritual; she didn't remember all the various traditions which had to be observed at a wedding.

'Would you go back home to Spain to get married?' Gina asked her curiously.

Irena hesitated. 'I've never thought about it.' But she knew her mother and brothers would expect it; their family pride would be offended if she did not get married in the local church where she had been baptised and made her first communion. Their village was fiercely religious, the dim, shadowy interior of the church always glowing with candles lit by the women of the village for some reason or another. The church was still the centre of their lives—they turned to God when they had nowhere else to go for help.

Esteban's deep voice said, 'Of course you would.'

Her startled grey eyes met his across the table; she felt the curious gaze of everyone else swing to watch them. She knew many of these people by now by face and name, but she was still a little tongue-tied in their presence, especially when Nick Caspian was there. He was such an important man; rich, powerful, remote from her world. She tried to picture him in her home, in her village, and couldn't. Irena did not feel she fitted into Nick's world, either, but Esteban did, she realised suddenly.

Esteban was at home here in England, and, of course, he would look just as right in her village in Spain. He had the ability to move from one world to another and be natural in either, like a chameleon which changed colour to suit whatever background you placed it against.

Yet underneath that adaptive quality there was another layer of Esteban's nature. One thing about him stood like stone: his love and grief for his dead wife. Nothing, it seemed could alter that. Esteban would never love again, or forget the darkness brooding at his very centre.

He had told her as much, brutally, the night he took her out to dinner. He had been warning her off. Hot blood stung Irena's cheeks as she realised what that meant—Esteban knew she was attracted to him and he wanted to make her see that she would only be wasting her time. It had been honest of him, and kind, and if she had any sense she would forget all about him.

'I expect your mother would want you to be married from home, wouldn't she?' Roz said, smiling at her. 'One day I'd like to see your farm, Irena, and meet your mother again. I have only the dimmest memories of her, but I know I liked her.'

Irena gave her a grateful look. 'She'd love to see you, Roz, she said so in her last letter. Our house is very small, and I suppose it is quite primitive by your standards—we don't have main drainage, and we often have power cuts, but you would be very welcome, they would really be happy to see you.'

Roz gave her a warm smile. Maybe she and Daniel should make a trip to Spain instead of staying in England? It would be fascinating to meet Grazia and her two sons, and see the little mountain farm where Irena had grown up. It would help her to understand Irena better. They had had such different lives, but they shared the same father, the same blood, and Roz was increasingly fond of her half-sister. She wanted to know what had made Irena the way she was.

Then she shivered, her eyes briefly closing. But that would mean flying, and Roz could not bear to fly at the moment. She hadn't liked to tell Daniel the chief reason why she preferred to stay in England for this holiday. She had yearned for the English countryside while she was on the plane in Cyprus, it was true, but that wasn't the whole truth. If they went to Mauritius or the West Indies, it would mean going by plane, and Roz couldn't face it. She knew that if she had to walk on to a plane she was likely to feel a wave of panic and run off again, screaming, or sobbing, which would be a humiliating experience. If that happened, she would never be able to look Daniel in the face again. How could she continue in a career as a foreign correspondent when she had become terrified of flying?

It could mean the end of everything she had worked for all these years, and she was secretly afraid of what it might do to her relationship with Daniel, too. Oh, he would be quite happy if she gave up her career, Daniel would like her to be in London with him, working together, in the office, going home together every night— but she wouldn't be happy. On the contrary, she knew she might grow bitter, full of resentment at losing something which had always been the most important thing in her life. She might start blaming Daniel, feeling that he was her enemy, because he had wanted her to give up her dream of being as good as her father one day. Rationally, she knew it wasn't Daniel's fault, it had been fate which put her on that plane, it had been fate that she should go through that ordeal, fate that she had been shot. It was fate, too, that she now felt this terrible panic at the very thought of flying. But she and Daniel had always fought over her job, and she knew herself well enough and was honest enough to admit that in her anger and disappointment she might well let reason fly out of the window, and turn on Daniel.

The dancing started an hour later, when all the speeches had been made and the tables had been cleared. Everyone settled down in groups, the lights were turned down a little and the music changed, too. Hazel and Piet went out on to the centre of the dance-floor, to noisy clapping and cheering, and ceremonially danced together, her veil flowing around, her skirts brushing the floor as she was whirled around, Piet's arms tightly possessive around her waist.

Irena watched them with a faintly envious smile—they looked so happy. Hazel had a glow today, a radiance she had never had before. She felt Esteban stirring in his seat and glanced at him through her lashes, hoping he was going to ask her to dance. He stood up, but he did not even look at her, he walked away and a moment later Irena saw him dancing with a blonde girl in a candy-pink dress which fitted her like a glove down to her knees when it exploded out into a cascade of pink frills to her feet.

Irena looked down, her hands trembling in her lap. She had no claim on Esteban; no right to be jealous, or hurt. He wasn't her property, he could dance with anyone he liked.

She had seen the blonde girl before; what was her name? Valerie something or other. She worked in editorial, and Irena had noticed her with Esteban once, but then she was very noticeable. It wasn't just her blonde hair or her striking violet eyes, or even her figure. It was the way she moved; it breathed sex. When she walked past all the men stared. Did Esteban find her sexy? Irena flicked a glance through her lowered lashes. The other girl liked Esteban, as she had observed last time she saw them together. Tonight, Valerie was making no secret of it, dancing much too close to him, her body sinuous, like a cat's, moving against him in perfect rhythm with the music. She was a good dancer, and so was Esteban, which didn't surprise Irena. He had Spanish music in his bones; the beat of the flamenco, the dark passion of hot summer nights.

Irena sipped her rather flat champagne, feeling depressed. How soon could she go home?

Philip Slade came over to ask Gina to dance, but before he arrived at their table Nick was on his feet, his long fingers curling around Gina's wrist to pull her up.

'Come on, dance with me.'

'There's no need for a caveman act!' she complained, but she hadn't noticed Philip heading their way, so she let Nick put his arm round her waist and move her on to the dance-floor.

Philip stood stock still, scowling after them. He had not seen much of Gina lately; he was beginning to wonder if she was avoiding him.

Roz and Daniel had observed the little incident, and they grinned at each other. 'Oh, poor Philip,' said Roz, tongue in cheek.

'Poor Philip,' Daniel repeated. 'You would think by now he would have worked out that he can't win—he might as well give up! Nobody ever has won against Nick Caspian, and if anyone ever does it will not be Philip Slade, I think.'

'It might be Gina, though,' said Roz thoughtfully, and Daniel made one of his very Gallic faces, something between a grimace and a shrug.

'Maybe. But she is a woman, and with a guy like Nick women tend to give in, not fight him. It's men who try to play hard ball with Nick.'

'Gina could, if she had to,' said Roz.

'You think so?' Daniel surveyed Gina's slender body, revolving in Nick's arms. 'She looks such a little thing to be so formidable!' he murmured with a touch of sarcasm which Roz heard perfectly clearly.

'She's a woman!' she said in a dry voice, and Daniel laughed.

'This is true. Such lovely red hair, such eyes, green as a cat's, and a mouth made for love. Yes, she is a woman, no question about it.'

Roz surveyed him coldly. 'I don't like the way you talk about her; you sound much too interested!'

He grinned teasingly. 'I'm not blind!'

'How would you like to be?' she threatened.

Daniel held up both hands in a gesture of submission. 'No, thank you. I was only joking. You know I prefer my women small and dark and hot-tempered.'

'Drop the plural,' said Roz. 'You only get one woman, Daniel, and don't you forget it.'

'Yes, your highness,' he said, laughing, then more soberly said, 'But what makes you think Gina could defeat Nick when everyone else fails?'

'Because she has Nick at a disadvantage,' Roz said wryly.

'Because she's a woman?' Daniel was amused and incredulous. 'Don't ever think it, darling!'

'Because Nick wants her so badly he's helpless,' Roz said calmly, and Daniel's jaw dropped.

'What on earth makes you think...?'

'I've watched them together, especially since I got back. It's as plain as day what is going on between them.'

Daniel stared across the room to where Nick and Gina danced. Nick's hand was moving slowly up and down Gina's back, but she was resisting his attempts to pull her closer, and when Nick put his cheek down against hers she moved her face away, her body rigid. Nick's skin grew darkly flushed, dragged tight over his cheekbones, his mouth tense with temper and frustration.

'Well, well,' said Daniel. 'I knew Nick fancied her, but I hadn't realised it was getting serious—what sharp little eyes you've got! It does look as if you could be right. Trust a woman to spot something like that!'

'We notice things more than men do,' shrugged Roz.

'Some things,' he accepted. 'But is Gina interested in someone else? Is that why she's giving Nick the red light?'

Roz gave him a derisive look. 'Sometimes I wonder why I love you, you blind bat. Gina isn't interested in anyone else. I'd say Nick Caspian has her whole attention.'

'Oh, it's a game plan?' guessed Daniel, frowning. 'Is she hoping to get him to marry her? She'll be lucky; a lot of other ambitious ladies have tried and failed. Nick has far too good a time as a bachelor to want to settle down with one woman. I expect he will, one day, when he decides it is time to get an heir, but she will probably be very rich and very well-connected. It won't be a love match.'

'You may be right, and I don't say he's thinking of marrying Gina—after all, he could have got the *Sentinel* as a wedding present if he had married her when Sir George was alive, but he didn't, although he was paying Gina a lot of attention then. But as far as she's concerned, I'm pretty sure she would never marry Nick Caspian. She hasn't confided in me but I'd say the way she treats Nick has more to do with the Tyrrells than any deep-laid plot to get Nick to marry her. Gina was always the loyal type. She loved that old man; she's never got over the sudden way Sir George died, and she still resents Nick for that take-over struggle, and the way he won—and I know she's more and more furious with the way Nick is changing the paper.'

Daniel pulled a face. 'She has a point. This was a serious, quality newspaper; it's changed out of all recognition and I can't say I'm happy about it, even though I expected it from the beginning. Nick is in the newspaper business to make money.'

'And you approve of that?'

'I accept it as a fact,' Daniel said crisply. 'As soon as he took over, he started going for higher circulation, and there's only one way of doing that—move down market. That's where the big sales are. Quality papers make it on advertising, not sales. The circulation battle is being won—the sales are climbing all the time, we're on our way to two million, Roz. Gina can't stop the process now and she won't win a fight with Nick—he's too clever and ruthless.'

'Maybe,' said Roz. 'But you're talking about business, and there are other sorts of war, and other ways of fighting. My money is on Gina. I think she's driving him crazy, but she's staying as cool as a cucumber. That's the way to win a fight—let your opponent defeat himself but never lose your own cool.'

'Poor old Nick,' Daniel said slowly, and there was no amusement left in his face. In fact, he looked taken aback, almost shocked. He was staring at Gina as if he had never seen her before in his life. Daniel was seeing her suddenly in a new light.

He had always liked Gina Tyrrell, admired her because of her family loyalty to her dead husband and his grandfather, Sir George Tyrrell. Daniel's French soul approved of that family loyalty; he saw Gina as a very feminine woman, loving and faithful.

Roz was aware of all that; she knew Daniel too well not to understand the way he thought, and she even wondered at one time whether Daniel might not be attracted to Gina, because of those qualities. Daniel had compared the two of them, she was sure, and wished she were more like Gina. He was disturbed by her own desire for an adventurous career; it wasn't, he thought, a girl's place to follow in her father's footsteps. She should want a more feminine role. In fact, Daniel felt threatened by modern women. Well, not any more, if that look on his face was anything to go by.

He had just discovered that Gina was not quite the female, yielding creature he had taken her to be, that Gina could be as ruthless, and obstinate, in her way, as Nick Caspian.

A twinge of pain shot through her shoulder, and she winced. She was beginning to feel tired. The wedding had used up most of her spare energy. Out of the corner of her eye she suddenly noticed Irena's pale little face, and frowned. Irena didn't look as if she was enjoying herself. Everyone else on the table had gone off to dance, leaving her alone without anyone to talk to.

Roz was about to call Irena over to join her and Daniel when another idea hit her. She whispered, 'Ask Irena to dance, darling, she's been left on her own. I should have noticed before, she looks very fed up.'

Daniel sighed. 'Do I have to? I like your little sister, but I'm not in a dancing mood, and, anyway, I don't want to leave you here alone. Why don't we ask her to come and talk to us?'

'Because she's dying to dance,' Roz muttered, pushing him. 'Look at her wistful expression! Go on! I'm OK, I'll enjoy watching.'

Daniel gave another sigh. 'What bullies women can be!' But he obediently went over to Irena, smiling as if it had all been his own idea. 'Roz won't dance with me—will you, Irena?'

It was tactfully put, as if she would be doing him a favour, and Irena fell for it, hook, line and sinker. 'I'd love to,' she said, her face brighter at once. She looked across at Roz. 'Are you sure you won't dance with him?' she called.

'Can't, darling—it would be a very painful exercise, with this shoulder, not to mention my arm!' Roz pointed out. 'Take him away, Irena, and teach him how to dance. He never learnt and it can be quite painful when he steps on your feet. Notice, I'm not giving him any recommendations!'

Irena laughed, but, as she found a moment later, Daniel was, in fact, quite a good dancer, light on his feet and unselfconscious moving around the floor. Irena enjoyed dancing with him, her long dress rustling around her legs as they spun. She was wearing one of Roz's dresses because she had not felt able to buy a new one for the wedding, and Roz had insisted on lending her a dress. It fitted her quite well, they were both very slightly built, but the rich sea-green silk was a stronger colour than Irena would ever have chosen for herself, and the way the dress clung made her very self-conscious. That wasn't the most embarrassing point—the neckline was rather low. All evening, she had been very aware that it allowed a glimpse of her breasts, so she had worn a triple gold chain to hide as much as she could.

'When do you have to be back in Paris?' asked Daniel as they spun across the floor.

'In four weeks' time now. The time has flashed past— what with Roz being hijacked, and so much happening...'

'Do you expect Des back by then?'

She looked wry. 'I wish I knew!' She looked up into Daniel's dark eyes, her own anxious. 'He is safe, isn't he, Daniel? You don't think we should be really worried about him? Roz says he often drops out of sight, when he's working, and it may be weeks before he gets in touch; do you think she's right?'

'I'm sure she is, Roz has grown up knowing that Des is not a nine-to-five man, you can't rely on him to write or phone home every few days. He's over there to find out what makes Vietnam tick these days, and so he's trying to absorb as much about the country as he can, Irena, and that means shutting out everything else. One of his great gifts as a foreign correspondent is his tunnel vision, his ability to forget himself and his world while he focuses on what's around him. I'm sure that Des is too busy to bother about us, and he'll have no idea at all that you might be worrying about him.'

Huskily, Irena said, 'But don't you think he should realise? I mean, if he cared about us, wouldn't he know we could be worried?'

Daniel looked over her head towards Roz, his face wry. 'Yes, it's a form of selfishness, I suppose, but it is what makes Des so good at his job. He simply sheds his own life, places, people, memories like a shell, and that leaves him open to every new experience he meets.'

'Is that what you were like, when you were a foreign correspondent?'

'More or less,' he admitted.

'And Roz?'

He shrugged. 'She hasn't had time to acquire the technique yet, but I'm sure she would.'

Irena sighed. 'Well, I hope you're right, and Des isn't ill, or in any danger!'

Daniel looked at her, kissed her lightly. 'I'm sure he's OK, Irena.'

Irena smiled back at him, grateful for the kindness in his voice and face, but a second later, over his shoulder, her eyes met Esteban's and she flinched at the coldness in his face, looking hurriedly away again. She was glad that the music swirled to a finish soon after that, and they could all walk back to the table.

As they reached it a uniformed hotel porter hurried up, an envelope in his hand. 'Is there a Miss Olivero here?'

Irena stopped in her tracks, startled. 'Yes, I am...I mean, I'm Miss Olivero.'

'Telephone message for you, miss—we tried to page you, but got no reply. They were from abroad, said it was urgent.'

'From abroad?' Roz interrupted. 'Vietnam?'

The porter shook his head. 'Couldn't say, I'm afraid. I didn't take the message, I'm just delivering it for the operators.'

Irena slowly came forward and took the envelope from him, tore it open with shaky fingers, while Roz and the others watched her intently. Esteban didn't take his eyes off her, but it was Nick who automatically tipped the porter.

'Thank you, sir,' the man said, hurrying off.

Irena read the words which seemed to dance up and down because her hands were trembling so much.

'Is it Des?' Roz burst out, her voice hoarse.

Irena looked up, white-faced, her grey eyes huge and dilated. 'No. It's my mother. She's been taken ill; Ramón wants me to come home at once. It must be serious. I must go.' She crumpled up the message, trying to think clearly. 'I . . . I must get a plane . . . will there be a flight today? I must ring the airport and——'

Nick interrupted. 'My private jet is ready to take off at a moment's notice. I'll get in touch with my pilot and tell him to get you there as fast as he can file a flight plan and have it agreed. No need for you to worry about ways and means of getting there. My driver is outside— he can take you to Roz's flat, to pack, and then take you on to the airport.' He frowned. 'You shouldn't really go alone, though.'

Roz stiffened as Nick looked at her, knowing what he was about to propose, and losing all her colour at the idea of stepping aboard another plane. Fear almost paralysed her, but Irena was her sister, she had grown very fond of her, so she took a long breath, summoning up her last reserves of courage, and said huskily, 'I'll go with her, of course.'

'No! You aren't up to travelling again, yet,' Daniel said at once, frowning.

'I'll be fine,' she protested, trying not to show how little she wanted to go.

'No, Daniel is right, stupid of me not to remember what you've just been through!' Nick said. 'You are in no state to go flying to Spain!'

'I'll go with her, I'll be happy to,' Gina quietly offered.

'You?' Nick scowled.

'I don't need anyone, really, please don't bother,' Irena whispered, wishing they would all stop arguing and let her go.

'She needs someone with her who speaks Spanish,' Esteban coolly intervened. 'There will be all sorts of details to deal with, once she gets to Spain. She'll have to get from Málaga Airport through the Sierra Nevada, and the fastest way would be to hire a car at Málaga Airport, and drive through the mountains, but that's a hard journey and she's far too upset to cope with all that. I'll take her—if you can spare me for a few days?'

Irena's heart sank.

Nick Caspian's frown cleared away. 'I should have thought of you right away, Esteban! I'll see to it that your job is covered while you're away, don't worry, and thank you, that's the perfect solution.'

'No, really, I don't need anyone to go with me!' protested Irena, appalled by the very prospect of Esteban travelling with her. 'I'm not a child. I flew here on my own, I can go back on my own!'

'Don't argue, there's a good girl,' Esteban said curtly. 'I'm going with you. You can't be allowed to travel alone, you're far too upset.'

'No! I don't want you to come!' Irena was a little flushed now, her grey eyes brilliant with distress and anger.

'Whether you like it or not, I'm coming, so don't waste any more time arguing,' Esteban said coolly, and, conscious of all the watching eyes, the attentive circle of people listening to everything they said, Irena fell silent, biting her lip.

If he was determined to come with her she knew better than to think she could stop him—but how could she bear all those hours of being alone with him, knowing that he had only come because he thought of her as a child needing his protection, not a woman needing something very different from him?

# CHAPTER NINE

NICK'S private jet got Irena and Esteban to Spain while it was still light, although the sun was sinking into the sea in a blaze of fire as they set off on the overcrowded coastline road which ran from Málaga airport through mile after mile of seaside resort towns, past high-rise apartment blocks, hotels, *pensions*, cafés, shops and neon-lit amusement arcades. Esteban kept his eyes on the road, from necessity, because there was so much traffic that a second's inattention could be fatal, but from the frown between his brows she knew he disliked the modern muddle of new building sites, cluttered streets and bumper-to-bumper traffic as much as she did.

'Tourism has a lot to answer for!' he muttered, and she agreed.

'But we aren't as poor now as we were before the tourists came!'

'No, that's true, but why do we have to put up with so much ugliness along with the jobs and the higher standard of living?'

'Maybe we should have fought the developers long ago? My mother says that after the Civil War people were burnt out; too tired to do anything but try to survive. Life was very hard for her family, when she was small, and it was the same for everyone else in Spain— and so when tourism started we didn't realise what it would all mean, we weren't quick enough to see the problems, we just saw the jobs and the bigger pay packets and a chance of a good life at last.'

'I'm afraid she's right.'

He fell silent, and Irena let her lids droop. It was a relief to close her eyes on the puzzlement of life. She had the car window beside her wide open; soon a cool breeze was blowing across her hot face, she smelt pines and olive trees and knew that they were turning inland, driving into the foothills of the Sierra Nevada. Slowly, she drifted into sleep.

Her head slid sideways and rested against Esteban's shoulder. He looked down at the top of her smooth brown hair, moved his arm gently and let her head fall against his chest, then enclosed her in his arm carefully so as not to wake her.

Her long hair blew across his face, and he brushed it down, smiling, letting the silky strands trickle through his fingers like water. They smelt of lemons, a scent he had always loved since he was a small boy and his mother had used to send him to pick lemons from their own tree. He liked to dig a nail into the rough skin and feel the juice spurt out, leaving that wonderful smell on his skin. He lifted his hand now, and inhaled the fragrance of Irena's hair on his skin, feeling the past link with the present in an instant's leap.

The car drove on and on along the winding mountain roads. On one side of them was a vertiginous drop—Esteban occasionally glanced over the flimsy barrier at the sheer fall of the mountains down to the green valley far below. There were few trees now, as they climbed higher and higher; the occasional thorn tree bending the way of the prevailing wind, or a pine tree in a sheltered hollow. There was little topsoil here, hardly any grass, just the silvery grey of the rock and a few clumps of gorse.

He could not drive fast, in the darkness; he did not know the road and was afraid of going off the edge into the abyss below. Irena woke up with a start two hours later, and heard a muffled beating right under her ear.

Then she felt the arm around her, and her eyes flew open. She was lying against Esteban, her face pressed into his warm body, too close for comfort.

Her heart turned over and over, and she sat up, flushed and trembling, conscious of him watching her.

'Feeling better?' he asked.

'I . . . yes, I suppose so, thank you. How long have I been asleep?'

'A couple of hours.'

She was appalled. 'You should have woken me up!'

'You obviously needed the sleep, so I left you. There was no need for both of us to stay awake. I could hardly lose my way on this road. There hasn't been a turning off for miles, except downwards over the edge!'

Had she been cuddling up to him all the way? Irena could have sunk through the floor, her face stinging with shamed heat. She sank back into her seat, keeping her distance from him.

A short time later Esteban drove into a village, shuttered and sleeping, with no street lights, the spire of the church piercing the dark midnight sky. There was one winding street, and then he slowed at a crossroads to study the road signs. He looked down at her, raising one black brow.

'How much farther, and which way?'

'Another half an hour to our village. The road is easier from here. We're through the mountain pass. You take the right-hand road and keep going.' She looked at her watch. 'I hope Ramón and Miguel aren't asleep.'

'Nick said he would get a message to them to tell them you were coming, and if Nick says he'll do something it gets done.' Esteban gave a suppressed yawn. 'I shall be glad to get there. I could do with a few hours' sleep myself.'

She was horrified at once. 'You're tired? Of course, you must be—shall I take over? I can drive, and I know this road.'

'No,' he said forcefully. 'I'd rather drive. These roads are pretty hair-raising. You may know them, but you're tired, it's the middle of the night, and you're upset. Not the best of moods to be in when you're driving on unmade roads. I'll be fine. How close to the village is your farm?'

'Another fifteen minutes' drive,' she said, watching his hands on the wheel. They had a wiry strength that moved her. She felt he could do anything he put his mind to. 'Why don't you let me take over? I'd like to, really!'

'No, thanks,' he told her curtly.

'But——' she began and he snapped at her then.

'I said no!'

She flinched visibly and didn't say another word.

There was a heavy silence for a minute, then Esteban gave a rough sigh. 'Irena, I'm sorry, I shouldn't have bitten your head off. My only excuse is that I'm very tired. I know that's not good enough, and you can tell me what you think of me tomorrow, but don't argue with me any more tonight. Let's just get you home, shall we?'

She didn't say another word until they were driving along the unmade track that led to the little farmhouse in which she had spent most of her life. The dust churned up under their wheels, she could hardly see through the muddy windscreen by now and leaned out to look.

Moonlight glittered on the tossing silver leaves of the gnarled old olive trees that grew on the dusty slopes behind the house, gleamed on the dark torches of the cypress, and the white walls of the house, walls built so thick that they kept out the strongest winds, the most driving rain. The windows were shuttered, no light showed, but the dogs woke up and began to bark, a donkey brayed, a sleeping stork sat up in his nest on top of the barn and clacked his bill angrily in protest at being disturbed, and in answer to this a mule in the barn below began kicking with his hind-legs at his stall.

'If Ramón and Miguel are here, they'll know we've arrived!' Esteban said drily, as he parked close to a bed of lavender which was still heady with the heat of the day's sun. Irena's mother dried it and sewed it into bags to put in closets and drawers, and hang inside their clothes.

Irena stumbled out of the car, stiff after hours of sitting in one position. She had been on edge to get here and find out what was wrong with her mother, but now that they were here she was too scared to walk towards the house, too frightened of what her brothers might have to tell her.

'Come on, let's go and find out what's wrong,' Esteban said gently, putting an arm round her to guide her. She felt his strength flowing into her and lifted her chin. She mustn't be such a coward! She had to be brave, for the sake of Ramón and Miguel. They might have left school, they might work on the farm, but they were still only boys, and their panic-stricken call for her to come home had to mean that they needed her.

The door was flung open before she took another step and Ramón came out, in crumpled jeans and an old shirt.

'Irena! Is that you?' he called in Spanish, peering into the shadows through which they moved.

'Yes, Ramón,' she called back, hurrying towards him.

Miguel appeared behind his brother, looking equally tousled and weary. Both boys had clearly been sleeping in their clothes.

'How's Mother?' she asked before she got to them and Ramón answered hurriedly, his voice reassuring.

'She's going to be OK, now, no need to worry.'

She gave a husky sigh of relief, until he added, 'They did the operation four hours ago.'

'Operation?' burst out Irena, her grey eyes opening wide. 'What operation? What's wrong with her, Ramón? How serious is it?'

'Her appendix almost ruptured; she had to have it out in an emergency operation, and it was touch and go whether the surgeon would be in time.' Ramón sounded tired. He yawned, running a hand through his thick black hair. 'They told me I ought to send for you, so I rang up the number you gave us on the newspaper, and they told me you were at some wedding, and gave me the number of the hotel. It took me ages to track you down, and cost a fortune. Mama is going to scream when she sees the bill.'

'Don't worry about it, I'll pay,' she said, and hugged him, ruffling his black hair. 'You look terrible, Ramón. I tried to ring you back, before I flew here, but there was no reply.'

He kissed her cheek and hugged her back. 'We've been at the hospital all evening, I didn't want to leave until I knew she was going to be OK.'

She looked searchingly into his pale face. 'And she is? You're sure?'

He nodded. 'They said she was out of danger and we needn't worry any more.'

Irena sagged, sighing. 'Thank God.'

'Did I do right, to call you, Irena?' Ramón asked anxiously, his boy's face older suddenly, tightened by adult responsibility and fear.

'Yes, you were quite right,' she said firmly. 'I'm so glad you did.'

His face tightened. 'When I called I didn't know if she would get through the operation, you see, and I knew you would want to be here if... well... if anything happened.'

'I'm proud of you,' she said, kissing him again.

Miguel was waiting for his hug. As she turned to him, he grinned. 'We'd still be at the hospital if this bossy sister hadn't thrown us out. She was a real gorgon, she kept talking to us as if we were just little kids!'

'Whatever gave her that idea?' teased Irena, and he laughed. Miguel was just sixteen, although he was strong for his age. He almost cracked her ribs with his bear hug.

'Well, she wasn't so old herself! Just because she had a uniform and a sister's cap she thought she could order us around just as she liked!' Miguel flexed his muscles. 'I'm no kid. I'm as strong as Ramón any day!' he boasted, and she wouldn't be surprised if it was true. She would swear he had managed to grow even in the short time since she last saw him, he was taller than her now, and broader, a muscled bull of a boy with a deep chest and a sturdy look.

Ramón was staring suspiciously at Esteban, who had held back tactfully, to let them greet each other.

'Who is this?' Ramón asked her. 'A taxi driver? Is he waiting for his fare?'

She flushed, stammering slightly, which was stupid and she could have kicked herself. 'No, no, Ramón, this is Esteban Sebastian, a friend from London. Esteban, this is my brother Ramón, and my younger brother, Miguel. Can we give him a room for the night, Ramón? He is very tired. He just drove me here, all the way from Málaga. It was very kind of him, I'm very grateful, and he ought to get some rest now we're here.'

Ramón frowned his doubts about this stranger who had appeared with his sister in the middle of the night. He met Esteban's implacable dark eyes, and the two of them stared in silence, measuring each other, like bulls before they clashed.

Esteban put the boy's mind at rest. 'I work for the newspaper where your sister has been translating this summer, and since I'm Spanish and know the terrain our boss asked me to escort Irena here. He didn't want her to travel alone, especially as she would have to drive from Málaga through the mountains at night, and since she's so young he did not think that was a good idea.'

Ramón soberly nodded. 'He was quite right, I should have realised ... But I panicked, I'm afraid.'

'Perfectly understandable, with your mother so very ill,' reassured Esteban. 'Any man would feel the same.'

Ramón widened his shoulders, a little flush of pride on his high cheekbones. 'Well, I thank you, on behalf of my mother, and myself.' He held out his hand, and Esteban solemnly shook it. 'Please, come inside,' Ramón invited him, leading the way into the white-walled living-room.

It was traditionally furnished with pieces which had been inherited from their father's parents along with the farm; a black Spanish oak dresser along one wall hung with copper pans and brightly painted china, an old well-scrubbed table, a matching high-backed wooden bench by the fire with wine-red velvet cushions scattered along the seat. Almost floor-length red velvet curtains hung on either side of the windows, and on another wall hung framed sepia photographs, taken around the turn of the century, perhaps, of their father's Olivero ancestors. They faded year by year, yet somehow you were at once impressed by their sharply individual faces; by Great-Grandfather's narrow moustache above his full lips, his proud black eyes and the look of fatalism in his high cheekbones and brooding stare, by his wife's lace bonnet and collar, her stubborn mouth and the loving, possessive arm which gathered up her five children where they stood in front of her and held them like hostages against oblivion.

Their mother had never wanted to 'modernise' the room, she loved it the way it was, although she had added some touches of her own—she had sewn the red velvet cushions and curtains, although they had replaced almost identical but faded ones. She liked to have vases of fresh or dried flowers around the room, scenting the air; she had bought an old glass-fronted Spanish cabinet at the local market, filled the top shelf with china and glass and brass, and the rest of the shelves held books in English and French. Grazia had not given up on her study of foreign languages, even though it had been a struggle sometimes to find time for reading.

They had a television set now, of course, and the two boys loved to have it on, but when she was alone in the house Grazia preferred to read and listen to music.

'Have you eaten? Can we get you some food?' Ramón asked, stifling another yawn.

'No, I'm not hungry. I think I'll go to bed right away,' Irena said. 'What about you, Esteban? Are you hungry?'

'No, I ate on the plane. I need sleep more than anything else.'

'Then I'll show you to your room.' Irena was taking over her mother's place; she turned to Ramón and said, 'I'm afraid you two boys will have to share a room tonight. Esteban can sleep in the big room.' She meant their mother's bedroom and the two boys exchanged looks, startled, but nodded, realising that there was no other room available for Esteban.

They had each travelled light, Esteban brought their overnight bags in and then Irena took him to the large main bedroom, where she had been born, as had her two brothers. This room, too, was very traditional; the bed was large and Victorian, with brass fittings, and the curtains were heavy cream lace, bought from the woman who made the lace and sold it at country markets all over that part of Spain. By the bed a red glass lamp glowed, giving the room a warmth which Irena had always loved. By day it was quite different, the white-washed walls more ordinary, but tonight they shimmered red, like a ruby.

'If you want anything, Ramón and Miguel are next door,' she said as he looked around the room. 'The bathroom is across the corridor. I'm afraid you'll find it rather primitive by your standards.'

He turned and smiled down at her, put a caressing hand around her anxious face. 'Stop worrying so much about little things! It looks like home to me.'

She trembled, closing her eyes as his fingertips lightly stroked down her cheek. 'Esteban...' she murmured, and then they both heard her brothers in the corridor, and Esteban's hand fell at once, he moved away.

'Goodnight, Irena.' His voice was deep and dark, like the night outside, and Irena fled to her own room and closed the door, trembling.

When he looked at her like that her pulses leapt and roared, and she felt light-headed. Just now she had thought he was going to kiss her again, and that terrible hunger had come back. She had stared at his mouth and ached to feel it touch her own. The pain of her frustration was unbearable.

When she was away, Miguel used her room, but, knowing she was coming, he had already shifted all his stuff—tapes, shirts, socks, posters of pop stars, underpants, the usual litter which lay around his room day and night waiting for their mother to tire of telling him to tidy up, and do it herself. For once, Miguel had done his own tidying up, and Irena's bedroom was immaculate.

There was a tap on her door and the two boys put their heads round. 'Want anything before we get back to sleep?'

She shook her head. 'No, I'm going straight to sleep. See you in the morning.' She smiled at them both with love. They were good boys, her mother always said, and she was right. They were. They had stepped into their father's shoes and run the farm, and they looked after their mother devotedly.

'Goodnight,' they both said, leaving on tiptoe, the old floorboards creaking under their feet.

Irena washed and undressed and got into bed. She put out the lamp and lay in the darkness of the shuttered room, listening to the Spanish night, the whirr of cicadas, the rustle of olive trees, the sigh of cypress, the harsh shriek of an owl hunting in the valley.

While she waited for sleep she heard Esteban's bed springs creak as he got into bed, heard him turn over, heard his sigh as he settled down.

It had felt so right, waking up in his arms in the car, on the way here. With her eyes closed she could almost believe she could hear the beat of his heart under her cheek, the warmth of his body close to her.

They both got up late next day. Irena was first, and found a note from Miguel saying that he and Ramón had had to start work; there was always a host of chores to do on the farm, especially as harvest time approached.

Irena found some of her mother's home-made bread, some fruit and some cheese, and set the table for breakfast, but just as she was going to wake Esteban he walked in, his black hair damp and his face freshly shaved.

'Sleep well?' he asked, smiling at her, and she nodded. 'Did you?'

'Like a log.'

He looked at the table. 'This looks very good.' He sat down and she poured him coffee, watching him choose the food he wanted, put it on his plate. He ate sparingly; a thin sliver of this cheese and that, a peach, some crusty bread.

'When do we visit your mother?' he asked, as he peeled the furry skin of the peach and the juice spurted all over his long, thin brown fingers. He licked one, absently, looking up at her, and her nerve-ends stirred with sensuality.

'Visiting hours are from two o'clock to four,' she said in a husky voice.

'Then I shall take a walk around the farm, with the boys, and have a chat with them,' Esteban decided. He leaned back, his dark eyes brilliant. 'I like your home,

Irena, and your brothers. I can see they love you very much.'

'I love them,' she said simply. She picked up the coffee-pot to refill his cup, but as she leaned over he moved away from her, sharply, as if he didn't want her too near him. It was like a slap in the face. She hurriedly poured the coffee to get away as soon as possible, and the spout splashed hot liquid over her bare arm.

She gave a cry of pain and quickly put the pot down, hurrying towards the sink to run cold water over the burn.

Esteban exclaimed angrily. 'My God, what have you done to yourself now?'

Tears stung her eyes. 'Nothing, leave me alone,' she muttered, holding her arm under the cold tap.

Esteban came over and took hold of her arm, staring down at the redness spreading on the delicate skin.

'You could have hurt yourself seriously! You must be more careful!'

She turned her head aside to brush the tears away before he saw them, but he caught the movement out of the corner of his eye, and groaned.

'Irena! Don't!'

'I'm sorry,' she whispered huskily.

He lifted her arm to his mouth, she felt a feather-light kiss on her scalded skin and her breath caught, audibly.

He frowned, looking up at her. 'Did that hurt?'

She looked back, her heart in her eyes. 'Every time I see you it hurts,' she said, and saw his face stiffen and pale.

'You mustn't say things like that!'

Hot colour crawled up her face, but she didn't look away. 'It's true, though.'

'I'm flattered if you have a crush on me, Irena,' he said bleakly.

'It isn't just a crush!'

'You're too young for me, Irena. I couldn't bear it if you got hurt, and I might end up hurting you if we don't stop this now! Forget you ever met me. I should never even have taken you out to dinner that evening.'

'Why did you?' she challenged from the depths of her hurt, her voice unsteady.

'I had a crazy moment,' he muttered and her spirits lifted a little.

'Esteban, just because your wife died, it doesn't mean you can never be happy again!'

'I never said it did!' He picked up a clean towel from a rail by the sink and delicately dried her arm. 'How does that feel? Better? Keep the towel round it for a while, keep it from the air.'

He was changing the subject, shutting her out again. 'Yes, thank you,' she said with such desolation that he looked at her and gave another little groan.

'Irena, listen—I am not going to repeat the same mistake twice. I'm not marrying a young girl, and then leaving her at home all the time, so that she gets bored and unhappy. If ever I marry again she'll be my own age and have a career, we'll probably work together, so that we see a lot of each other.'

'I want my own career! We all do, these days. Your wife may have stayed at home in Madrid and felt lost, but she was a different person. I went to live in Paris on my own, when I was eighteen, after living here, miles from anywhere—and I soon found my feet. I came to London on my own, didn't I? And I've been working at the *Sentinel*, exploring London by bus, making friends. I haven't hidden at home, too scared to venture out!'

He was staring at her grimly, those dark eyes fixed and formidable, and she bit her lip, but she had to say these things to him, to make him see the mistake he was making.

'I'm not your wife again!' she protested. 'I'm me, a different person. You can't live in the past, or keep repeating it. And, anyway...' She lifted her head in a defiant movement, her long, silky hair flowing over her slender shoulders. 'Who mentioned getting married? We don't know each other yet. Why can't we just be friends?'

Esteban caught her flushed face between his hands, staring down at her. His eyes held a sad mockery. 'You know why.'

Her heart missed a beat. 'Do I?' she whispered innocently, but she wasn't fooling him.

He moved a hand down her neck, softly touched her breast, and she trembled at the sensual caress. 'Yes, you do,' he murmured, staring at her parted, quivering lips. 'I'm already half in love with you; it's too late for us to try being friends!'

Irena's heart nearly stopped. She instinctively raised her head, going on tiptoe because he was so much taller, and Esteban's mouth swooped down in a hungry, searching movement, their bodies coming together as if magnetised.

She heard the rough intake of his breath as she put both arms around his neck, her fingers thrusting into his thick black hair to pull his head down closer. His mouth was hot and demanding, his hands caressed her slowly, sensuously, and she quivered with passionate response. She had never known her body could feel such pleasure; it was a revelation to her. Through her lashes she saw that he, too, had his eyes closed, and his face was blind and taut, darkly flushed.

He kept telling her she was a child, but she was a woman, and she knew he wanted her so much at that moment that he was shuddering, his thighs hard against her, his body fully aroused. She knew because she was experiencing the same driving desire. She had never felt anything like it before, this intricate puzzle of love and need and anger and passion. But she knew what it was; and she was convinced now that Esteban felt the same.

But he wasn't ready to admit it yet. Esteban was a stubborn Spaniard who had made up his mind years ago, in bitterness, never to love again, and he did not easily change. All the same, he needed to love and be loved. Everyone did. She did. He was the man she wanted, had wanted from the minute she first set eyes on him in that plane, and she was sure Esteban wanted her, too, even if he was having a problem admitting it.

He suddenly pushed her away, his eyes open, glittering. 'I must go and find your brothers,' he muttered, but he didn't move for a minute, he stood there looking at her, passionately, and Irena put her hand up to his mouth and ran a finger along the strong lines of it.

'You wouldn't want anyone else to be my first lover, would you?' she softly said.

His eyes flashed. 'No!' he said with explosive force, his body tense.

She gave a satisfied sigh, and Esteban observed her, narrow-eyed. 'You little witch-child! How do you know these things? With those big, innocent eyes and that shy little smile?'

'I'm a woman, Esteban! Lots of girls from my class at school are married with babies; some of them have two or three children already! My best friend, Pilar, married at sixteen! I didn't. My mother wanted me to go to university, because she had given up on her own career, so she wanted me to have it for her.'

He frowned. 'You mean you don't want a career?'

'No, that isn't what I mean. I want one, but so far I haven't quite decided what I want to do. I don't want to be just a housewife and mother, though. I've learnt too much since I started travelling. Well, being at university is very eye-opening, you know. I've had boyfriends, I've been kissed.'

Esteban did not look delighted with this news. She gave him a smiling look.

'And, before you ask, no! I've never been to bed with anyone.'

He said through his teeth. 'I was not about to ask, but since you've brought the subject up, why haven't you?'

'Because I never wanted anyone enough to take the risk of getting AIDS or ending up pregnant. If I had fallen in love, things might have been different.' She looked at him through her lashes, her grey eyes a glimmer of invitation, and smiled.

'You take my breath away,' he said, suddenly laughing. 'I'm going to find your brothers before you get me down on my knees proposing!'

Only when he had gone did she realise what he had said and her heart missed a beat. Did Esteban understand what he had just admitted? It had been a joke, but it showed the way his mind was working. There was a crack in the monolithic façade. Irena sang as she cleared the table and washed up, tidied the kitchen and then whisked round the house with a vacuum cleaner and a duster.

They drove into town after lunch. The men insisted on helping Irena wash up before they left.

She had cooked their meal. *Patatas a la riojana*—an easy dish, a casserole, cooked in the oven in a dark red earthenware pot, just layers of sliced potatoes, tomatoes and onions with peppers and local *chorizo*, their village version of Spain's favourite spicy sausage. She served this with some rolls she had baked at the same time, and as a sweet they ate fruit from the big fruit bowl, piled high with pomegranates, oranges, peaches, apricots and slices of watermelon.

The boys talked to Esteban while they ate; she automatically took on her mother's role, hardly said a word, watching all the time to make sure they had enough food, their glasses were always refilled with the locally made red wine which was their usual table drink at lunchtime. It was rough stuff, but far from being strong; a child could drink it, if it was watered down. Their mother had always given them wine and water when they were small, although they had their own spring of clear water coming from deep inside the rocks, and could safely drink as much as they liked.

'It's good to have you home,' Miguel said, grinning. 'I was afraid I would have to cook our meals, or, even worse, eat Ramón's cooking!'

She gave him a wry look. 'Nice to know I'm appreciated, even if it is only as a stand-in for Mama.'

The boys both laughed loudly. 'A woman's always handy around the place,' said Miguel.

When they reached the hospital, run by nuns from a local convent, the same order who had run her convent school, Esteban stayed in the waiting-room with the boys while she went in to see her mother alone. Grazia had been put in a small side-ward; her bed was the only one occupied for that moment. She lay in the immaculate bed, eyes closed, hands on the coverlet, so still, so neat, that Irena stopped, staring, fear clutching her heart.

There was no sound of breathing.

'Mama . . .' she whispered.

Then the lashes stirred and the lids lifted and her mother turned her head on the pillow to look across the room at her, frowning as if the movement hurt.

Irena ran to the bed. 'Oh, you are awake!' She bent to kiss her and that close she heard the slow drag of her mother's breathing. 'How do you feel? Is there anything I can get you?' she chattered, to cover her fear and anxiety. 'I brought you flowers from the garden, and some fruit.'

Grazia looked at the bunch of flowers held out to her, her jaw dropping. 'You picked my white roses!'

They were her favourites, their petals like snowflakes, pure and white and untouched until the summer rain or mildew came and spoilt them. It was not easy to grow roses in that heat, that sunbaked soil; Grazia kept them in terracotta pots and moved them inside on bad nights, saved every drop of water for them, fed them, pruned them, laboured over them obsessively.

Irena had known she might annoy her mother if she cut some of them. Quickly, she said, 'They wanted to come.'

Grazia stared, eyes wide with stunned surprise at that. 'What?'

'They wanted to be with you!'

Grazia seemed to hesitate between rage and laughter, and then in the end chose to laugh. She had always had a strong sense of humour, and adored nonsense books, like the English novel *Alice in Wonderland* which she had read to her children when they were very small.

'You crazy girl. Rubbish! I spend hours every week to make sure my roses give me blooms like these, and you calmly cut half a dozen!'

'You couldn't see them from here, and they were just perfect,' Irena calmly said. 'Another day or two and they would be past their best. Another week and they would be dropping petals all over the path. And the boys said you couldn't come home for a week at least! So I brought them to you so that you could see them before they died.'

Grazia touched one with a gentle, caressing fingertip, looking at the rose and smiling. 'They are perfect, aren't they? You're right, I'm glad you picked them. I would have hated to come home and find they were all blown. Roses are like children, you know. You lavish love and care on them, but so much can go wrong however hard you try to protect them. The wind may blow them to shreds, frost may scorch them in the bud, you can get mildew or rot or greenfly, and a host of other threats. I suppose that's why we love them, because we know that the odds are always against us.'

Irena drew up a chair and sat down. 'Tell me about your operation.'

Grazia grimaced. 'I don't remember anything about it, but it's very difficult to move about now. They tell me it will get easier and in a few days I'll be leaping about like a cicada, but in the meantime every time I move I feel my stitches drag.'

'How horrid. But thank heavens the boys got you here in time. It's such a difficult drive, too. It must have been like a fairground ride!'

'You know what the road here is like!'

'We bumped about all over the place coming here.'

'The boys didn't bring you in that awful old truck of theirs?'

'No, Esteban drove us in the car he hired at Málaga.'

Grazia sat still, looking at her daughter. 'Esteban?'

Irena blushed. 'Oh . . . I forgot to mention . . .'

'Yes, you did,' said Grazia, but she was smiling. 'He's Spanish, obviously, but where did you come to meet him, and why did he come home with you?'

'He's the marketing director of the *Sentinel*.' Irena stood up. 'He's outside now, with the boys. Can I bring him in to meet you?'

'Wait a minute, wait a minute!' Grazia said, looking concerned. 'He sounds important. Marketing director? How old is he? He must be much older than you. What is going on between you and him?'

Irena went to the door. She wasn't ready to confide in her mother yet. 'You'll like him, I know you will.'

'Irena, come back here, answer my questions,' Grazia called after her as she opened the door.

Irena looked into the corridor to signal to Esteban and the boys, and then she froze in her tracks, her mouth opened in a gasp of shock.

'You come back here, girl,' Grazia said from the bed. 'I want to talk to you!' Then she, too, saw the man whose face had so startled Irena, and she stopped talking.

She was very familiar with that face, of course, but seeing him when she had not expected it seemed to have taken her breath away.

He was casually dressed as always; in old stone-washed jeans and a loose blue tunic top, like a French labourer, and wore trackshoes on his feet. In those clothes if you didn't look too closely he could be any age from forty onwards, but he was much older than he looked. Still a very attractive man, though; silvered dark hair, blue eyes, a very lived-in face with those lines of humour and experience, warmth and tolerance, around his eyes and mouth.

'Des! Oh, Des! Where have you been?' Irena threw her arms around him and hugged him. 'I'm so glad to see you!'

'Good to see you, too, sweetheart,' Des said, kissing her nose. 'You looked washed out, and no wonder! You've been leading a hectic life since I saw you off at Charles de Gaulle airport, haven't you?'

She laughed unsteadily. 'You've no idea what it has been like! But what on earth are you doing in Spain when we all thought you were in Vietnam?'

'I was in Vietnam. I got back to London early this morning. I'd been making my own way, trying not to make contact with too many Europeans, I hadn't seen a newspaper or heard a broadcast for days, so I hadn't heard the news, but I abandoned my tour after I got a telegram from Nick Caspian, one of hundreds he seems to have sent, trying to track me down.'

'He's nothing if not thorough!' Esteban said from the doorway. 'You have to give him that! No stone was left unturned.'

Des grinned. 'Well, he found me under the last stone he turned. One of his cables finally reached me, and I immediately started home.'

'Have you seen Roz?' asked Irena. 'She looks so fragile, didn't you think? It was a horrible experience, she has lost a lot of weight, and I think it has left her with some strain, not surprisingly. She isn't sleeping very well, although they've given her sleeping pills.'

'I know, I saw her this morning. She told me you were here, and about your mother's appendix, and I decided to follow you on a scheduled flight. I've driven here straight from Málaga—Nick told me Grazia was in this hospital.'

He turned towards the bed, smiled at the woman in it. 'Hello, Grazia. How are you now? Feeling better than you did yesterday?'

She politely held out a hand. 'Hello, Mr Amery, yes, I'm much better now, thanks.'

Irena felt very odd. These two polite strangers shaking hands were her parents. It was hard to believe. Their brief contact had had such far-reaching results, like a small stone thrown into a pond, and then sending out ever-widening ripples. They had met and been lovers for a short time. If they hadn't she would never have been born. These two had contributed the genes which went to create her own separate individuality. They had met and then parted for twenty years. Now here they were, making small talk about the weather, joking about the hospital food, discussing Vietnam.

'You have two wonderful sons—I've been talking to them out there, while Irena was with you,' Des said and Grazia glowed, as she always did when people praised her boys. She was a loving mother.

Irena hung back to let them have some privacy while they talked, but out of the corner of her eye she was watching her mother, seeing the faint colour which had invaded her pale face since Des appeared, the new brightness of her eyes. Grazia was a good twenty years younger than Des; she was still a very lovely woman, with her gleaming dark hair, olive skin and rounded figure.

Esteban put a hand under Irena's elbow suddenly and steered her out of the room. The corridor outside was empty and she looked from one end to the other.

'Where are the boys?'

'They went to get a coffee. They'll be back in half an hour to see your mother.'

Esteban was grinning to himself, looking suddenly younger, almost carefree. 'Your family are like a box of exploding crackers. You never know what is going to jump out next. This is quite a surprise! Did you expect Des here? From what you said, he and your mother were...well, just a short fling and then goodbye.'

'It wasn't like that,' she whispered, appalled in case Des and Grazia might have overheard him.

They walked out of an open door, into a little garden, with a lawn and beds of flowers. Bees buzzed heavily to and fro, the scent of lavender filled her nostrils. She stood, rubbing her hand against the purple flowerheads on their long stalks, while she talked about her parents and her own perception of their relationship.

'My mother was in love, I think, although I'm only guessing, but Des was unhappy, he drifted into a relationship just to escape his own sadness. My mother realised that in the end, so she went away, not knowing she was expecting me by then. But she was happy with my stepfather, you see. I know she was, they were contented with each other. It wasn't the same sort of feeling at all, she never loved him the way she had Des, but they had a good life. I don't really think she ever forgot Des, though—or why would she have sent me to him like that? I think I was a sort of love token she sent him.'

Esteban listened, face intent. 'Do you think he realised that?'

She gave him a rueful smile. 'I can never guess what Des is thinking, I don't think he wanted to pick up where they had left off.'

'He's here now, isn't he?' said Esteban drily.

Her face changed, startled. 'Yes, he's here. I wonder what that means?'

Esteban watched her thinking about it, absorbing the possible implications. 'Do you mind?' he asked, and she shook her head.

'No, I don't think so.' But she had a faintly mournful look, and Esteban frowned.

'Afraid of losing out with both of them if they come together?'

It was a shrewd guess, and she bit her lip, laughing rather crossly. 'A little, maybe. Childish and selfish of me, isn't it?'

'No, just human,' Esteban said, his fingers softly stroking her cheek. 'None of us likes changes, especially where those we love are concerned. We always expect everything to go on day after day exactly as it always has been. It's an inbuilt human instinct.'

Irena gave him a laughing look. 'Talking about me, or yourself, Esteban?'

'Both of us,' he said, his arm going round her waist and dragging her towards him.

Her heart began to beat wildly.

'I knew you were dangerous to me the minute I saw you on that plane from Paris,' he said huskily. 'I kept watching you out of the corner of my eye and thinking how lovely you were, but I was afraid of getting involved, especially with a girl so much younger. And I'm right—it's madness to think of it!'

Irena wasn't listening, she was staring into those dark eyes of his, reading their emotions, and trembling.

'I love you, Esteban.' She was exposing her vulnerability to him, giving him the chance to hurt her, if he chose. It was the gift love always gave.

He groaned. 'We haven't known each other any time at all, and I can't take advantage of you. I ought to give you time, plenty of time, to be sure of how you feel.'

She wanted him so badly to kiss her. She watched his mouth as he spoke, sighing. 'I'm sure,' she said with utter certainty.

'We shouldn't rush into anything,' he said, running his lips down her throat.

'No, darling,' she said, her eyes closing.

'You're so young, Irena. You've hardly had a chance to meet many men.'

'I don't want anyone else!'

'But——'

She put a finger on his mouth. 'Stop talking, Esteban.'

'Darling,' he murmured, and then his mouth was on hers and Irena forgot everything else but him. From now on, she knew, her life was going to be rooted in Esteban as it had always until now been rooted in Spain, in the farmhouse where she had been born, in the family she loved so much. From now on, they must take second place, though, because Esteban was always going to come first.

Don't miss *Playing Hard To Get*, Barbary Wharf Book Four.

Esteban and Irena have found that it's far better to "make love, not war," but what of Gina and Nick? Will they ever reconcile their differences? And now that Valerie Knight has lost Esteban, will she give the ever-persistent Gib Collingwood a chance to prove himself? Find out in *Playing Hard To Get*, Barbary Wharf Book Four, coming next month from Harlequin Presents.

HARLEQUIN PRESENTS®

# BARBARY WHARF

Charlotte Lamb is one of Harlequin's best-loved and bestselling authors. Her extraordinary career, in which she has written more than one hundred books, has helped shape the face of romance fiction around the world.

Born in the East End of London, Charlotte spent her early childhood moving from relative to relative to escape the bombings of World War II. After working as a secretary in the BBC's European department, she married a political reporter who wrote for the *Times*. Charlotte recalls that it was at his suggestion that she began to write "because it was one job I could do without having to leave our five children." Charlotte and her family now live in a beautiful home on the Isle of Man. It is the perfect setting for an author who creates characters and stories that delight romance readers everywhere.

BARBARY WHARF
#1498  **BESIEGED**
#1509  **BATTLE FOR POSSESSION**

**HARLEQUIN HISTORICAL**
# CHRISTMAS
**·STORIES·1992·**

Capture the magic and romance of Christmas in the 1800s with HARLEQUIN HISTORICAL CHRISTMAS STORIES 1992, a collection of three stories by celebrated historical authors. The perfect Christmas gift!

Don't miss these heartwarming stories, available in November wherever Harlequin books are sold:

**MISS MONTRACHET REQUESTS by Maura Seger
CHRISTMAS BOUNTY by Erin Yorke
A PROMISE KEPT by Bronwyn Williams**

Plus, as an added bonus, you can receive a FREE keepsake Christmas ornament. Just collect four proofs of purchase from any November or December 1992 Harlequin or Silhouette series novels, or from any Harlequin or Silhouette Christmas collection, and receive a beautiful dated brass Christmas candle ornament.

---

Mail this certificate along with four (4) proof-of-purchase coupons plus $1.50 postage and handling (check or money order—do not send cash), payable to Harlequin Books, to: **In the U.S.:** P.O. Box 9057, Buffalo, NY 14269-9057; **In Canada:** P.O. Box 622, Fort Erie, Ontario, L2A 5X3.

---

**ONE PROOF OF PURCHASE**

Name: _____

_____

Address: _____

_____

City: _____

State/Province: _____

Zip/Postal Code: _____

HX92POP                                        093 KAG

# "BARBARY WHARF" SWEEPSTAKES
## OFFICIAL RULES — NO PURCHASE NECESSARY

**1.** To enter each drawing complete the appropriate Offical Entry Form. Alternatively, you may enter any drawing by hand printing on a 3″ × 5″ card (mechanical reproductions are not acceptable) your name, address, daytime telephone number and prize for which that entry is being submitted (Wedgwood Tea Set, $1,000 Shopping Spree, Sterling Silver Candelabras, Royal Doulton China, Crabtree & Evelyn Gift Baskets or Sterling Silver Tray) and mailing it to: Barbary Wharf Sweepstakes, P.O. Box 1397, Buffalo, NY 14269-1397.

No responsibility is assumed for lost, late or misdirected mail. For eligibility all entries must be sent separately with first class postage affixed and be received by 11/23/92 for Wedgwood Tea Set (approx. value $543) or, at winner's option, $500 cash drawing; 12/22/92 for the $1,000 Shopping Spree at any retail establishment winner selects or, at winner's option, $1,000 cash drawing; 1/22/93 for Sterling Silver Candelabras (approx. value $875) or, at winner's option, $700 cash drawing, 2/22/93 for the Royal Doulton China service for 8 (approx. value $1,060) or, at winner's option, $900 cash drawing; 3/22/93 for the 12 monthly Crabtree & Evelyn Gift Baskets (approx. value $960) or, at winner's option, $750 cash drawing and, 4/22/93 for the Sterling Silver Tray (approx. value $1,200) or, at winner's option, $750 cash drawing. All winners will be selected in random drawings to be held within 7 days of each drawing eligibility deadline.

A random drawing from amongst all eligible entries received for participation in any or all drawings will be held no later than April 29, 1993 to award the Grand Prize of a 10 day trip for two (2) to London, England (approx. value $6,000) or, at winner's option, $6,000 cash. Travel option includes 10 nights accommodation at the Kensington Park Hotel, Continental breakfast daily, theater tickets for 2, plus round trip airfare and $1,000 spending money; air transportation is from commercial airport nearest winner's home; travel must be completed within 12 months of winner notification, and is subject to space and accommodation availability; travellers must sign and return a Release of Liability prior to traveling.

**2.** Sweepstakes offer is open only to residents of the U.S. (except Puerto Rico), and Canada who are 21 years of age or older, except employees and immediate family members of Torstar Corp., its affiliates, subsidiaries, and all agencies, entities and persons connected with the use, marketing, or conduct of this sweepstakes. All federal, state, provincial, municipal and local laws apply. Offer void wherever prohibited by law. Taxes and/or duties are the sole responsibility of the winner. Any litigation within the province of Quebec respecting the conduct and awarding of a prize may be submitted to the Régie des loteries et courses du Quebec. All prizes will be awarded; winners will be notified by mail. No substitution of prizes is permitted. Winner selection is under the supervision of D.L. Blair, Inc., an independent judging organization whose decisions are final. Chances of winning in any drawing are dependent upon the number of eligible entries received. All prizes are valued in U.S. currency.

**3.** Potential winners must sign and return an Affidavit of Eligibility within 30 days of notification. In the event of non-compliance within this time period, the prize may be awarded to an alternate winner. Any prize or prize notification returned as undeliverable may result in the awarding of that prize to an alternate winner. By acceptance of their prize, winners consent to the use of their names, photographs or their likenesses for purposes of advertising, trade and promotion on behalf of Torstar Corp. without further compensation to the winner unless prohibited by law. Canadian winners must correctly answer a time-limited arithmetical question in order to be awarded a prize.

**4.** For a list of winners (available after 5/31/93), send a separate stamped, self-addressed envelope to: Barbary Wharf Sweepstakes Winners, P.O. Box 4526, Blair, NE 68009.